ACCOUNTING FOR LOVE

A LONG VALLEY WESTERN ROMANCE NOVEL – BOOK 1

ERIN WRIGHT

WRIGHT'S ROMANCE READS

To my own cowboy:
Thanks for being my biggest cheerleader, and for putting up with me, even on launch week

CHAPTER 1

STETSON

July, 2016

S TETSON MILLER LOOKED around his father's cluttered office. Well, it was Stetson's office now, although he was sure it'd *feel* like his dad's office until the day he died.

Died like his father had.

Stetson pushed the thought away. His office, his father's office…none of that mattered now. Not with the office, the house, and the whole damn farm about to be stolen from him.

Desperate to do *something*, even if it was wrong, Stetson turned towards his father's desk, ready to start filing papers or straightening up or something.

Shit.

Piles were everywhere – piles on top of piles. He was pretty sure piles were having little baby piles every time he turned his back on 'em. He picked up a sheaf of papers with a heavy sigh, thumbing through the jumbled mess. Hmmm...they appeared to be his heating bills for the cow barn this past winter...

Stetson looked up from the papers to stare at the rows of drawers to his right, all labeled in his father's spiky, neat handwriting. *Cow Expenses*, the far right drawer label read, a little newer than the other labels. Not quite as yellowed. Not quite as faded. Stetson went to shove the papers inside when he noticed another drawer labeled *Heating and Cooling Expenses*.

He paused, eyes darting between the two drawers. The receipts really could go in either one...

Stetson dropped the papers on top of a precarious pile of receipts with a muttered curse that would have his mother spinning in her grave. He pulled his hat off and chucked it in the corner, shoving his hands through his hair.

This was ridiculous. The whole thing was ridiculous. Since when was a *farmer* supposed to like paperwork? Everyone knew that *real* work was done out in the fields, not in an office. Bucking hay, building fences, castrating cows – now *that* was a job well done.

Pushing papers around was for pansies. People who couldn't hack it out with the real men.

Stetson's eye fell on the letter in the center of his father's desk. It sat there alone, unsmudged, no scribbled phone numbers or coffee spills on it. It mocked him with its pristine state of being, in such stark contrast to everything else in the office.

Thirty-one days. The bank had given him thirty-one days to bring his loan current. He didn't need to re-read the letter to know what it said. Every word was imprinted in his brain, like a branding iron on his gray matter.

And it had been thirty-one days.

The month had passed in a blur, with Stetson considering and then discarding every idea he could think of, their outrageousness growing as the days passed.

He could sell his truck.

Except, what farmer didn't have a truck? How was he supposed to haul hay or workers or rolls of fencing out to the pasture? How was he supposed to *farm*? And to add insult to injury, selling his truck wouldn't actually solve the problem. That'd bring in $30,000, maybe. On a good day. Not $176,900.

Then came an even worse idea: He could ask Wyatt or Declan for a loan.

Which of course meant admitting that he'd screwed everything up from day one. Admitting that he was on the brink of losing the family farm.

The derision, the sneer on Wyatt's face when he heard the news…Stetson didn't need to actually tell his oldest brother the truth to know what Wyatt's reaction would be. It was the same reaction that Wyatt had for almost every piece of news Stetson had to relay – good, bad, or indifferent.

And this news was definitely *not* indifferent.

No, he couldn't tell his brothers. He couldn't

admit how much things had gone downhill since their dad died. They'd never forgive him.

Not, of course, that any of this was *his* fault. It was all the damn bank's fault. Why, his dad was hardly even cold in the ground. They didn't need to be circling like vultures overhead, just waiting for a chance to shred him to pieces. They could at least give a guy a chance to get his feet underneath him.

Stetson picked up the letter, unsullied by even a dirty fingerprint, and stared down at it unseeingly. Then, with a precision worthy of a surgeon, he began tearing it into strips. Long, straight, neat strips.

"When that asshole banker gets here, I'm gonna give him a piece of my mind!" Stetson growled to himself, tearing the letter into smaller and smaller pieces. Each tear of the paper was satisfyingly precise. "I'll teach him how *not* to be a bastard. I'll teach him with my fists, that piece of shit—"

A clearing of a throat cut Stetson off at the pass. He froze, hoping that if he just stood there long enough, no one would notice him. He'd blend into the background, like a cowboy version of a chameleon, and avoid the wrath of his housekeeper.

She cleared her throat again.

Dammit.

Stetson let the pieces of the letter flutter to the ground – his one act of defiance that he dared to do in front of his formidable housekeeper – and then turned to the doorway.

There Carmelita stood, her fists planted on her

hips, shooting him glares that Stetson could only be grateful didn't *actually* kill.

Behind his fiery, rotund Hispanic housekeeper stood…a woman?

Stetson stared.

She stared back.

Time stood still as Stetson's mind scrambled to put the information in front of him together into a coherent whole. The hated banker, the one he was going to beat into the ground with his fists was…a *woman*.

"That low-down snake!" Stetson erupted, staring at the *female* banker. "That piece-of-shit bank president sent in a *woman* to do his dirty work? Is he hiding behind your skirts? Huh? Why doesn't he come in here like a *real* man and face me?"

Carmelita's face, unhappy to begin with, turned a bright shade of red that Stetson hadn't seen since he'd gotten the oh-so-grand idea at age six to dye the white sheets in the guest bedroom a deep red. He'd used them as a cape to jump off the roof – he was gonna fly like Superman.

He wasn't sure which had hurt worse: His broken leg or being on the receiving end of *that* stare.

"This *lady* is going to look at your books," Carmelita ground out, staring Stetson down, which considering she had to crane her neck upwards to do, was quite the feat. His righteous indignation began to seep out of him like a balloon with a pinprick in it. "*And you will treat her like a lady!*" she thundered.

With that, his housekeeper moved to the side, letting the tiny woman through. Even with heels on, the banker barely came to Stetson's shoulder.

"Hi," the woman said, extending her hand toward him. "I'm Jennifer—" She stopped abruptly, Stetson noted with pride. Probably because he was looking down at her hand with all the respect he might give a rotting fish.

Good.

Maybe he couldn't punch the banker, and maybe he couldn't use choice words to tell her exactly what he thought of her chosen profession – stealing farms from hard-working, red-blooded Americans – so he'd do the next best thing: He'd put her in her place.

"I know who you are and why you're here," Stetson said flatly. "Let's get some things straight. First, you're not staying here. This is not a guest house; you can get a room in town. Second, this is *my* home, and I'll not have it invaded by…" he waved his hand in the air, "bank people. You can use the office and the bathroom. The rest of the house and farm is off limits."

Really warming up to the task of telling this woman what's what, he continued, "Third, I'm *not* paying for the privilege of having my farm stolen from me. If you have to make a phone call, you'll do it on your own dime. Use your damn phone, not mine. Fourth, Carmelita serves lunch at noon each day. Because I'm a good host, I'll let you eat one sandwich with a glass of water, but that's *it*. Finally, you're gonna start at 8 and be gone by 5 every day. No exceptions."

Drawing in a deep breath, he crossed his arms and glared down at her. Damn, it felt good to order the bank around. It was 'bout time they got a taste of their own medicine.

CHAPTER 2

JENNIFER

*J*ENNIFER STARED UP at the pissed-off farmer, towering over her, and had the most vivid — if short — daydream of stomping into his instep, kneeing him in the balls, and walking out the door. With that, she could go back to her boss, tell him that the farm had failed the audit and that the Miller Farm needed to be repossessed for lack of assets and income. It's what her boss wanted her to report back, anyway. Jenn knew that.

But she pushed down her urge to knock the asshole of a farmer down a peg or two, and instead forced a smile onto her face. An unconvincing, stiff-as-dried-plaster smile, but a smile nonetheless.

"Thank you for the information. Now, if you wouldn't mind, I have work to do, since it appears none has been done in months." She stared pointedly at a particularly precarious pile of file folders tottering on the edge of the desk and then back up at Mr. Miller.

Waaaay up at Mr. Miller. Dammit all, this guy was a giant. Were all Sawyer farm boys this tall? She was going to hurt her neck, craning it like this.

Not that she was going to admit that to this overgrown ape. She'd already had her fill of his condescending attitude and she'd only been in his presence for three minutes. She'd admit a weakness to him about the same time she'd chop off her right foot.

And anyway, it sure as hell wasn't her fault that her father wasn't cousin to Bigfoot.

"Whatever. I have *work* to do. *Real* work." He stomped past her and out into the hallway, his footsteps echoing with anger as he stormed out of the house.

Jennifer turned back to the portly older woman still hovering in the doorway, and shot her a more genuine smile. "Thanks for your help," she said.

"My Stetson should not have behaved that way," Carmelita announced angrily, her cheeks a flaming red. "I will have a talk with him when he comes back in about his manners." She too stormed down the hallway but her soft slippers didn't *clomp* nearly as loudly as Mr. Miller's boots had. Jennifer somehow knew that Carmelita was regretting her shoe choices that very moment.

Jennifer turned back to the office, surveying it with a groan. She'd audited some pretty disastrous offices before on behalf of the bank, but she was pretty sure that this one took the cake. In stark contrast to the rest of the pristine house that Jennifer had caught sight of as she'd followed Carmelita back here, this disaster zone really looked like it just deserved to be set on fire so they could start over again.

Why was it that offices run by men always looked like this? When women were the bookkeepers, the offices may not have been spick-n-span, but they were at least tolerable. But men's offices…it was like they were allergic to filing paperwork. Or cleaning.

Which was, of course, why the bank was sending her out to audit the books to begin with. People who were on top of their paperwork and their filing and their bills didn't tend to have their businesses taken away from them. That wasn't always true, of course – sometimes a business ran into a string of bad luck that couldn't be avoided – but usually, it was a hatred and/or a complete lack of bookkeeping knowledge that put people into this position.

She sighed. She knew from hard-won experience that getting grumpy about the state of an office at the beginning of an audit did her absolutely no good. It was time to get to work. She could complain about farmers' inability to file papers into a drawer later over wine with Bonnie.

Just as Jennifer moved to sit down in the rickety old office chair that looked like it'd survived a WWII bombing raid, she heard the front door slam open, footsteps echo through the entryway and hallway, and then Mr. Miller reappeared in the doorway, his face as brilliant red as Carmelita's had been. Avoiding eye contact, he snatched his cowboy hat off the filing cabinet in the corner – Jennifer hadn't even noticed it in amongst the piles of papers everywhere – shoved it down on his head, and then stormed back out, the door slamming shut behind him.

Again.

She wasn't sure if she wanted to laugh or cry.

She sat down in the office chair with a snort-laugh that ended with a yelp of terror when she found herself staring up at the ceiling, her head cracking against the hardwood floor as the chair slammed backwards. "What the hell?!" she half-yelled, the words coming out of her before she could stop them. She usually tried not to swear at a customer's place of business, but she also usually did not sit in chairs that fell over like fainting goats, either, so she figured she had a valid excuse just this once.

She rocked and rolled and finally heaved herself out of the chair and onto her feet, staring down at the innocent-looking chair with a baleful glare. She brushed her black skirt off, trying to get the bits of hay and mud and cow shit off her from her roll on the floor. That was *definitely* not how she wanted to start this audit. With a sigh, she hoisted the ancient office chair upright again, settling down into it gingerly this time, finding just the right spot to keep her precarious balance.

Yup, this was gonna be one fun audit, all right.

CHAPTER 3

STETSON

*A*FTER LAYING DOWN the law with that no-good *female* banker, Stetson stormed out towards the barn, remembering halfway there that he'd left his hat behind, went back to retrieve it, and then stormed out to the barn again, where he promptly spent the rest of the day hiding.

Well, not hiding, of course. He was a man. Men did not hide from women. He was just choosing to spend his day working on very important things that were *not* inside of the house, was all.

Which was a very different kettle of fish altogether.

His hired hands were working hard on vaccinating the new calves, and he really should go help them, but it wasn't fair to them if he made them pay for the bank's bullshit by biting their heads off for the heinous crime of breathing, so on second thought, he should probably stay away from them.

All people, actually. And anyway, Christian – his foreman – was out there with them, so he'd make sure that the men were doing what they needed to.

And while Stetson was staying away from people, he should probably do the same with beasts for that matter. Cows were trying enough on the best of days, and this was definitely *not* a best day, or even a mediocre day.

So, the barn it was. At least there, he had a reasonable chance of being left alone.

Damn the bank anyway. At least if they'd sent a man, he could've told that man what he really thought about him, the bank, and how screwed up this whole situation was, punctuated perfectly with his fists. To add insult to injury, Stetson also knew that he was going to hear about his rudeness – and swearing – from Carmelita sometime in the very near future.

The prospect of an ass-chewing didn't exactly make him jump up and down for joy.

Stetson looked around, trying to find a very important project to work on. The Miller Family Barn was more of a storage building and workshop combined together than a typical barn. In the winter, he would park tractors and other equipment in it to keep the expensive machinery out of the weather, but since it was the middle of summer, there was a lot more elbow room to be found.

Along one wall, there were workbenches, toolboxes, and all of the miscellaneous tools and junk that had accumulated over the years. The piles of stuff were ostensibly kept under the pretense that they could someday be used to make repairs, but Stetson knew better.

The truth was:

1. He was a farmer;
2. Farmers never threw away anything; and
3. Carmelita was never allowed into the barn.

There were some laws of nature that just shouldn't be broken.

And then, he spotted it. Hidden in the very back corner of the barn was a small tarp-covered tractor. Unlike the modern equipment that was used for the day-to-day operations of the farm, this tractor was nearly 60 years old.

It had belonged to the Miller family from the day it'd rolled off the assembly line. It was the first piece of motorized equipment Stetson's grandfather had purchased. Since then, a long line of equipment had passed through their ownership. Bigger, more efficient equipment cycled through as technology advanced, but the family had held on to this particular tractor as a reminder of all the things it symbolized.

Stetson wandered over to the miniature tractor — at least, miniature in comparison to today's beasts — and pulled the tarp off, sending up a cloud of dust that had him coughing and gasping for air. Once most of it had settled and the air became breathable again,

Stetson ran his hand over the rusty, chipped green paint and split leather seat, remembering…

Over the years, the tractor had sat in a field through rain, snow, and shine. Eventually, time took its toll on the machine to the point where it would no longer run. Then one day, Stetson's father wrapped a chain around the front axle, lifted a much younger Stetson into the seat, showed him how to release the clutch and how to steer, and together, they pulled the rotting tractor to the barn. It was the first thing Stetson had ever driven.

"What're we gonna do to Grandpa's tractor?" Stetson had asked.

"We're going to fix it," his father replied, amused at the obviousness of the answer.

"But this one's old and we have better ones over there."

"I guess that depends on how you judge better," his father had said, kneeling to look his young son in the eye. *"If it wasn't for this tractor, your grandfather wouldn't have been a successful farmer, and that means that we wouldn't have had the money or reason to buy those other tractors that you say are better."*

"But why are you going to fix it? The other tractors are stronger and faster."

"First, I'm not the only one who's going to fix this tractor, son. You're going to help me fix it. Second, we're going to fix this tractor because it's a reminder of where our family has come from. It's a symbol of all the hard work that's gone into giving us the things we have now. It may never plow another field, but this is the tractor that plowed the fields and planted the seeds that are your future and I want you to learn to respect that."

Stetson's vision was blurry. The tractor was fuzzy around the edges and his face was hot, but in his mind, he could clearly see the deep, sun-etched wrinkles at the corners of his father's eyes.

Stetson wiped at his eyes with the back of his hand as the memory faded. Damn dust in the air, anyway.

The tractor still didn't run. There was a new part attached here and there, but he and his father had only ever worked on the tractor a few moments at a time over the years.

"If they want my farm, fine. But this tractor will run again, by God," he said out loud. It was a declaration to the universe. Finally, something that he could *do*, rather than just sit and worry. What had thirty-one days of worry gotten him? A banker in his father's office, doing her damnedest to steal the Miller Family Farm.

He grabbed a wrench and got to work. Worrying and stewing over bankers solved nothing.

What about drooling over bankers?

Stetson stopped, his wrench in mid-air as he stared unseeingly at the tiny, antique tractor in front of him. Where the hell had *that* thought come from?

The stress was getting to him, that was for sure. If he didn't pull his head out of his ass, and soon, he was going to lose his mind along with his farm.

And Stetson wasn't quite sure which one was worse.

CHAPTER 4

JENNIFER

*J*ENNIFER GINGERLY stood up from the chair, rolling her neck from side to side to work the kinks out of it as she looked down with satisfaction at the piles of papers on the wooden, scarred desk. To the untrained eye, it would look a lot like it had when she'd started – just piles of papers laid out everywhere – but this time, there was a *purpose* for those piles.

Which definitely couldn't be said for the first set of piles she'd inherited.

She hadn't sorted out the piles elsewhere in the office, stacked on every horizontal surface available, but hey, baby steps.

Now that there was some semblance of order in the chaos, at least in the desk arena, she just had to find a way to help Mr. Miller save his farm, even if he was an ungrateful ass. He may not appreciate her hard work on his behalf, but that didn't mean it was any less her job.

Which, now that she thought about it, was rather like operating on a pain-in-the-ass patient and saving their life, whether or not they wanted the help, and whether or not they appreciated it.

Jennifer wrinkled her nose at herself. How was it that she'd gone from one profession to the next, and neither one of them appreciated the effort and care she put in? She must be a glutton for punishment – a masochist of the first order. There was no other explanation.

"Would you like a break now?" came Carmelita's voice behind her, startling her out of her self-pitying thoughts. She whirled around to face the door, her hand over her heart, a startled yelp spilling out of her.

"Sorry, I did not mean to scare you," the housekeeper said with a kindly smile. "You have been hard at work for a long time, though, and I thought that you might want to take a break."

Jennifer's eyes flicked to the elk clock on the wall. *Wow – 3:15 in the afternoon? Where did today go?* "I'd love that," she said. "You have my crust of bread and my glass of water to drink?"

She may or may not have said that with sarcasm dripping off every syllable.

Carmelita sighed as she turned to head back towards the kitchen, her soft slippers making her almost completely silent on the creaky hardwood floors.

"Stetson has not come back in from outside yet, but when he does, we will have a talk about manners," the housekeeper said over her shoulder in her softly accented voice. "He was not raised by his parents — God rest their souls," she crossed herself, "to speak to a woman that way. Or anyone at all."

They'd made it to a cheerful, if cramped, country kitchen, where Carmelita set about making a sandwich for Jennifer, her hands moving rhythmically between the ingredients. There was a small, worn table shoved up against the wall, so Jennifer slipped into a seat, watching the housekeeper at work. Homemade white bread, thick sliced roast beef...her mouth was watering at the sight.

"Are his parents no longer here?" she asked, trying to phrase that in the most tactful way possible. The housekeeper seemed intent on bringing them up, even if Jennifer usually didn't get involved or even know much about a client's background. But since Carmelita wanted to talk about it, it was only polite to respond and ask questions.

Nothing more than that.

"No," Carmelita said sadly, sliding a plate in front of Jennifer along with a glass of milk. Jenn stared at the glass in bewilderment — she hadn't been served milk to drink since she was a small child. She took a hesitant sip of the super thick, creamy liquid as Carmelita continued, "His mother died 14 years ago in a car accident — hit a deer on the way over to Pocatello to visit Stetson's older brother, Declan. His father was devastated; they loved each other very much. He never dated or looked at anyone else. He died of cancer last July, or so they say. I think he died of a broken heart. He was never right after Mrs. Miller died."

She stopped talking just as Jennifer had taken another overly large bite of her glorious sandwich – she'd almost just shoved the whole thing in her mouth because it was so damn delicious, but had settled on only taking a huge bite instead.

Which left her chewing furiously so she could respond without her mouth being full.

Awkwarddddddd…

Finally, she swallowed and said, "That's a really sad story."

Which was just about the most lame comment on the planet, but she really wasn't sure what else to say.

Carmelita pulled out an oversized mixing bowl and canisters, lining them up in preparation to make something delicious, Jennifer was sure of it. It was probably a good thing that an audit only lasted a couple of weeks. She was going to have to be rolled out the front door at this rate on a hand truck if all of Carmelita's cooking was as delicious as the sandwich had been.

She scrambled for something else to say as Carmelita hummed softly to herself, stirring flour and sugar together in the ceramic mixing bowl.

"So Mr. Miller has an older brother?" She wasn't sure why she was asking this question, other than out of politeness. It certainly wasn't any of her business.

She *certainly* didn't care.

"*Two* older brothers," Carmelita corrected, adding salt into the mixture. "Wyatt is the oldest and then Declan two years later. Stetson was...how do you say? Surprise." She laughed a little. "Mrs. Miller was so flustered when she found out she was pregnant again. Stetson was eight years after Declan, and they had believed that they were done. She wanted a little girl but of course, he was a boy. Mr. Miller was happy, though, and Stetson never left his side. As soon as he was out of diapers, he spent the whole day with his father. Never complained – his shadow. Two peas in a pod.

"Declan was always closest to Mrs. Miller, and Wyatt...well, I do not know. Wyatt is his own person."

Which was just about the oddest statement ever, but Jennifer didn't feel comfortable asking for clarification. She'd already gossiped about her client's past long enough. It was time to get back to work.

With a barely stifled groan, she pushed back from the worn kitchen table and stood, stretching for just a moment before smiling at the housekeeper. "Thank you for lunch," she said.

The housekeeper bobbed her head, flashing a quick smile before concentrating on her baking again. Chocolate chips were being added to the bowl now. Jennifer tried not to drool.

Too much, anyway.

"My Stetson – his bark is worse than his bite. He is just worried. He has a good heart. He will be nicer to you next time. I will make him."

Jennifer let out a snort of laughter at that. The diminutive housekeeper was probably a good two feet shorter than Mr. Miller, but Jennifer was pretty sure that in this case, size wasn't really what mattered.

"Well...ummm...thanks again," she said, and headed back to the office.

She was still pretty sure that Stetson Miller was a jackass of the first water, but at least he had good taste in housekeepers. That was one point in his favor.

Even if it was his only one.

CHAPTER 5

STETSON

S TETSON PULLED the alternator off the tractor and carried it over to a workbench. Covered in a thick coating of grease and dirt, it didn't look like much, but he was sure that with a bit of a tune-up, he could make it sing again.

Or at least put-put-put down the field. Wouldn't that be something – he could start using this tractor around the farm a little again. Machines were meant to be used, not to just sit around under a tarp.

"Hey, Stets, you here?" Declan's voice called out as the barn door squeaked and rattled open.

Dammit. What is he doing here?

Declan was certainly Stetson's favorite brother – it wasn't hard to be declared the winner in that contest, considering the competition – but that didn't mean he wanted him here on the farm. Not with the damn banker still here. It wasn't five o'clock yet, so she would still be in their father's office, doing her best to steal the farm away.

Stetson didn't want Declan anywhere *near* Jennifer-the-Thief.

"Hey, Dec!" Stetson called back, as casual as he could. "I'm back here!" He listened to his brother's cowboy boots echo on the dirty concrete floor, and then he appeared in the doorway, pushing his hat back on his head as he looked around the indoor riding arena that had long ago been turned into a large repair shop.

"Whatcha workin' on?" he asked, making his way through the random piles scattered about. He got over to Grandpa's tractor and let out a little laugh. "Is the farm doing so well, you don't need to worry about working out in the fields anymore? You can take a day to just work on this old thing?"

Stetson shrugged as he fiddled with a nut, pretending to be utterly fascinated by it. He couldn't meet his brother's eye. "I just...wanted to do something a little different today. Figured it was 'bout time someone worked on this."

"Yeah, Dad would've loved to see this up and moving again."

They both stood in silence, staring at the family relic. "So," Stetson finally said, clearing his throat and wiping his hands on a grease rag, "what's up?"

"Just wanted to stop by and talk to you about having a family meeting. Are you free on Friday afternoon? With the drought hitting hard this summer, Wyatt's dryland wheat is ripening faster than usual. I think he's anxious to get it out of the fields."

Stetson bit down on the inside of his cheek. Hard. Since Wyatt was the only dryland farmer in the bunch, his wheat always ripened first, which meant he always harvested first. Which meant he could always destroy farm equipment with impunity and then return it without a care in the world because he was cock-sure his brothers would fix it all before starting into their own harvests.

Which was true, mostly because they had no other choice.

"Wyatt...I just don't know," Stetson hedged, trying to figure out a way to get out of sharing farm equipment this year. "You know we haven't been getting along lately."

Or ever.

Stetson decided to leave that part out. "If I have to work with him on harvest again this year, I'm not sure we'd both still be alive by the end of it."

Declan let out a little laugh. They both knew it was true; Declan was just too nice to say it out loud. "C'mon, brother," Declan chided him, "you know it's what Dad would've wanted."

Which was also true, dammit. And it sucked that Declan was willing to play that card, even if it *was* true.

Of course, he didn't get the title of peacemaker in the Miller family for nothing. He'd been the liaison between his older brother and younger brother since the day Stetson arrived on the scene, and had finely honed his craft over the years. He was the only reason Stetson and Wyatt ever ended up in the same room together. Without Declan serving as a buffer between his two brothers, they would've either stopped talking to each other or killed each other long before now.

It was a toss-up as to which it would've been.

Stetson let out a long sigh. "Yeah. You're right. Fine. Meet me here on Friday? We'll go over our harvest schedules and put together a plan then." Hopefully the banker-a-la-thief would be gone by then.

He could only hope.

Declan grinned. "Awesome. See you then." He turned and started making his way back out of the barn, when he stopped and turned back. "What's up with the fancy car up at the house?"

Dammit, hell, shit, God almighty—

"Just an accountant I hired to come look at the books. You know, make sure they're in tip-top shape." He smiled, trying to act as casual as possible, but he was dying inside. There was *no way* Declan would fall for that one. It was the stupidest idea known to man. You didn't deal with paperwork; you just threw it in the office, closed the door, and ignored it.

Everyone knew that.

"Great idea! I'm proud of you for thinking of that. Having someone else take over the books is just what you need to do."

Or that. Declan could always think it was a *grand*

idea to invite a bookkeeper into their lives. Stetson barely kept from rolling his eyes. His brother had the most ridiculous ideas sometimes.

"Hell," Declan continued, "I might just go on up to the house and talk to him about coming over to my place and taking a look at my books. Do you—"

"Oh, you shouldn't bother her! Not ummm...not right now. Maybe later. But she has a lot to go through right now. Lots of...paper." He waved his hand in the air vaguely.

Shut

the

hell

up

Stetson gave Declan a weak smile.

"She, eh?" Declan arched an eyebrow teasingly. "Is she a looker?"

"Oh no. Ugly. Mole on her nose. A little hair sprouts out of it."

He had no idea where that came from. Or where any of this was coming from. He shouldn't be lying to his brother. He knew that. He also couldn't figure out how to tell him the truth.

And wasn't that just quite the pickle to find himself in.

"Damn. Well, I better get to work. See you on Friday." He walked out, his footsteps fading away, and then the creak and squeal of the barn door signaled his exit.

Stetson's shoulders dropped and he stared

unseeingly at the tractor in front of him. He'd just screwed up, and he knew it. He shouldn't have lied to Declan. His parents had raised him better than that.

But to tell him the truth? That was unthinkable, too.

With an angry growl at himself and the world in general, Stetson gathered up the rags he'd dirtied and carried them to his truck he'd left parked outside the night before. He'd drive the rags back up to the house and make sure that the banker wasn't doing something she shouldn't be. Like, snooping around the house, searching through trash cans or something, hoping to find incriminating evidence. Of what, he wasn't quite sure, but dammit all, she had shifty eyes. He'd seen that this morning. He shouldn't hide out in the barn any longer; he had to go protect his family's legacy.

Ummm…*work* in the barn any longer. Because he sure as hell wasn't *hiding*.

He was a man. Men didn't hide from women.

CHAPTER 6

JENNIFER

*H*AVING FINISHED the piles on the desk (and on top of the filing cabinet and in corners, lurking like monsters in a nightmare), Jennifer had moved on to the inside of the filing cabinet.

It wasn't a typical metal filing cabinet, but rather a beat-up wooden relic with rows of drawers, all neatly labeled in the same spiky handwriting that she'd found on a few papers scattered around. In contrast, most of the papers piled *on* the desk had been in a blocky handwriting, and Jennifer had spent the afternoon idly trying to figure out which handwriting was the father's, and which one was the son's.

She pulled a cabinet drawer open and found file folders, neatly labeled by year, tabs marching through the drawer like soldiers, and instantly knew that this settled it – the son's handwriting was the blocky one. All of the file folders in here had the spiky handwriting on it, and Jennifer was willing to bet next year's salary on the fact that Stetson wouldn't take the time to organize file folders if his life depended on it.

So when the father was alive, he filed and organized, and then once he died and Stetson took over, all of that stopped? Not surprising. The man she'd met that morning didn't give a rat's ass about paperwork or bills or filing, of that she was sure. Of *course* he'd let his paperwork fall into disarray, and then blame the bank for the mess he'd found himself in.

Men.

She started to reach for the first file folder in the drawer when she glanced up at the elk clock on the wall, the bull's head thrown back as it bugled to the world, a 2 on the tip of its nose. *Huh. It's almost five. If I get started in on another project, I'll be here hours past when I should be, and God only knows, the bank doesn't pay overtime. Plus, Mr. Miller was quite clear on my work schedule this morning.*

She shoved the drawer closed instead. She could get started on this phase of the excavation tomorrow morning. That would be soon enough. She began gathering up her laptop bag and notepad when her phone started singing out *Working Overtime.*

With a groan, she grabbed her iPhone and swiped to answer. "This is Jennifer Kendall," she said in her most professional tone of voice. It was how her boss wanted her to answer the phone, even though he damn well knew who she was.

Just one of his many idiosyncrasies.

"How shhhhsirifks ldislkds," her boss' voice chirped in her ear.

"Hold on, Greg, let me get somewhere with better reception." Jennifer hurried through the farmhouse and out onto the covered porch that stretched the length of the house.

"Can you hear me now?" Jennifer asked, feeling distinctly like she was starring in a Verizon Wireless commercial even as she said it.

"There you are. What took you so long?" Greg sounded annoyed, but then again, everything annoyed him.

"Sorry, I'm way out in the sticks. The signal isn't very good; I had to go outside."

"Whatever, just don't leave me waiting like that again," Greg huffed on the other end of the call. "Are you making progress?"

"Yes?" she said, more of a question than a statement. "I mean, I got through the piles on the desk today. I'll get to work on the filing cabi—"

"I don't need a play-by-play of your workday," Greg said, cutting her off. "I just need to know if they have the money. The Millers. Are they going to bring their loan current?"

"There's only one Miller who still lives here, first of all, and second, I have no idea. Like I said, I haven't even touched the filing cabinet yet and there's a lot—"

"I want results, not excuses!" Greg interrupted.

Again. Jennifer bit down on the inside of her cheek. Hard. There were days…

"Give me a few more days and I can give you more information," she said politely but firmly.

"I want a status report at noon tomorrow." And with that, he hung up.

Jennifer stared down at her phone in shock. Even for Greg, he was being inordinately pushy and difficult. He usually didn't hound her for a status report on an audit until she'd been there for a few days. He'd been in the foreclosure department of the Intermountain West Bank & Loan for longer than she had. He knew what he was asking for was impossible, so why the bee up his bonnet?

There was something not quite right here…

She heard the rumble of a diesel engine and looked up to see Mr. Miller pull up in front of the house, giant tires crunching on the gravel driveway, and then he hopped out, leaning back in to grab something. Unbidden, her eyes followed his legs up to the curve of his ass, his Wranglers cupping it just so – *damn, I can't breathe* – and then he straightened up, his hands full of…dirty laundry?

He sauntered towards the house in that loose-hipped swagger that all cowboys seemed to naturally take on at birth, up the two steps and onto the covered porch. With a nod of greeting, he shoved the rags underneath his arm to free up a hand to get the screen and front door open, and then stood back, allowing her to pass by him and into the house.

She headed back down to the office to grab her stuff, and she could swear she could feel his eyes on her ass every step of the way. Which was ridiculous, of course. He thought she was some awful creature, come to steal his farm from him. He certainly wasn't checking her out.

Just like she hadn't been checking out his ass. She'd just been studying the fashion trends in Wrangler jeans.

Which was a totally different thing.

She finished shoving her stuff into her bag, slinging it over her shoulder with a grunt at the weight. Someday, she was going to be able to afford a Mac laptop again, instead of these oversized bricks HP liked to call laptops.

She headed out into the hallway, where she promptly slammed right into Mr. Miller, who'd been heading…well, somewhere else. And now his hand was on her elbow and he was standing in front of her and looking down at her and she couldn't breathe again and…

CHAPTER 7

STETSON

*J*ENNIFER CRASHED into him just as he was heading to the guest bathroom to clean up. Instinctively, he reached out to steady her, and then his hand dropped like he'd been burned.

Don't touch the enemy!

He'd never felt so off balance in his life and he hated the feeling with a passion. He wasn't about to show weakness in front of this woman though, so just as instinctive as steadying her had been, he now looked down at his watch theatrically. "It's 5:05," he informed the stupidly beautiful thief in front of him, who was sadly *not* in possession of a single mole, hairy or otherwise, on her nose. Damn the bad luck. "Didn't I tell you to be gone by 5:00?"

Even as the words were leaving his mouth, he knew he shouldn't. He knew he was being an ass. But today seemed to be the day for saying things that he knew he shouldn't, and regretting them even as the words were coming out.

Well, at least the one thing he had going for him was consistency.

Her brilliant green eyes snapped open in shock and just as she opened her mouth to tell him her thoughts – in great detail, no doubt – Carmelita's voice thundered through the house. "Stetson Byron Miller!" she yelled, advancing towards them in the already crowded hallway. He tried shrinking up against the wall, but his cowboy-turned-chameleon act didn't work any better the second time.

"Your parents would be ashamed of you!" She poked him in the arm, glaring up at him, eyes flashing. He gulped. "You apologize to Ms. Jennifer —" She stopped and turned towards the thief in front of him. "What is your last name, dear?" she asked kindly, at total odds with the tone of voice she'd just been using with him.

Stetson wanted to thump his head back against the wall. Didn't Carmelita know that this woman was trying to ruin five generations of Miller farmers? Whose side was she on, anyway?!

"Kendall," the petite woman said politely, as if they were in a drawing room and being introduced over tea. Stetson glared down at her. She smiled angelically up at him.

"You apologize to Ms. Jennifer Kendall right now!" the housekeeper bellowed, not missing a beat as she turned back towards him, arms akimbo.

Stetson tried hard to stifle his groan. Voicing it would *not* help his case. "I apologize, Ms. Kendall, for my rudeness." He wanted so badly to end that with, "I should be kind to those who are trying to destroy my life," but somehow, through an inhuman act of self-restraint, he managed to swallow those words instead. He was rather proud of himself, really.

Jennifer seemed to be waiting for him to finish, as if she could sense there was more that he wanted to say, but when he stayed quiet, she nodded once in acceptance. "I will be here at 8 a.m. sharp tomorrow morning," she informed him cooly.

With that, she turned sideways and shuffled past him, heading for the front door. Stetson flattened himself against the wall again, but still, her body traced a sizzling hot line across his where they brushed against each other.

CHAPTER 8

JENNIFER

*J*ENNIFER DROVE DOWN the long gravel pit Stetson apparently considered to be a driveway, heading back towards town. She'd blown through Sawyer on the way out to the Miller place that morning, but it was time to find her hotel – no, *motel* – room and some food. In that order.

There was a huge, fancy hotel on the edge of town that Jennifer had first spotted online when making reservations for this audit, but the price per night…it was definitely geared towards tourists, *not* bank auditors. Greg would've laughed himself off his chair if she'd asked for a $250-per-night per diem for a hotel room.

So Drop-Inn Motel it was.

Please don't let the whole room be decorated with bugling elk.

She wasn't sure how many more of them her

fragile psyche could handle right about now. She sent the silent plea up to the heavens just as her phone buzzed in her bag. Keeping one eye on the gravel road as she fished around in her laptop bag, she finally snagged and pulled the vibrating phone out.

Paul Limmer, iMessages informed her.

Jennifer dropped her phone like she'd been scalded. *Paul? Paul?!?!?!*

"You do realize we're not dating anymore, right?" she said aloud, and then felt ridiculous for talking to herself. She could read his message in a minute and decide how to respond then. For now, she needed to concentrate on where she was going. She'd made it back to town surprisingly fast; the drive had felt much longer that morning. She looked around as she drove through the tiny town, smiling a little as she went. Quaint brick buildings lined Main Street, leading up to a stone monument in the town center, flowering petunias planted around the base. It was…adorable.

She came to a stop at the only stoplight she'd spotted thus far and waited for it to turn green. Compared to Boise and the Treasure Valley area as a whole, it felt like a portal through time to drive down these streets. At least traffic wouldn't be a problem with this audit. Honestly, no traffic and Carmelita's cooking were about all this audit had going for it so far.

She refused to admit that Mr. Miller's good looks were another plus towards the audit. Now, if he had a personality to *match* those good looks…

Eventually, she came upon the little motel, the low buildings lining a central parking lot. The Drop-Inn sign jutted out over the sidewalk and under the name, a smaller sign proclaiming "Color TV" creaked in the breeze, slowly swinging back and forth.

Jennifer studied the motel with a critical eye. It was straddling that fine line between quaint and rundown, and was teetering dangerously towards the later.

Please no elk decor, please no elk decor, Jennifer chanted to herself.

The hardest part of checking in was waking the little old lady in the rocking chair behind the counter. Once Margaret shook off the sleepiness, though, checking in was a simple matter of signing the guestbook. Jennifer was surprised when Margaret used an attachment on her iPhone to charge Jennifer's company credit card.

"We may be a bit rundown, dear, but we're not completely cut-off," Margaret said in response to the look on Jennifer's face. The cloud of blue hair bobbed up and down with Margaret's forceful nod for emphasis.

"Th-hank you," Jennifer stuttered, smiling politely as she accepted the key. An honest-to-God key with a heavy metal fob, the number "6" inscribed on it. She couldn't remember the last time a hotel gave her a real room key. Maybe never.

"I hear you're doing some accounting out at the

Miller place," the older woman continued, pinning Jennifer down with an inquiring stare.

"Oh, uh yeah," Jennifer stumbled, not sure how much this lady already knew, or how she knew it. Were all small towns like this? She wasn't sure if this was creepy or charming.

"Well, you set that boy straight. He's a damned hard worker, but I don't think he's very good at keeping the books. He'd much rather be out driving a tractor than running an adding machine," Margaret said, before wandering back to her television.

Obviously the "You're here to take his farm away" part hadn't been passed on to Margaret. Thank God for small favors.

Jennifer found the room easily enough. With only one floor and 15 rooms total, it wasn't exactly difficult. It was so close to the office, she decided to just pack her stuff to it instead of re-parking the car.

Within a few minutes, she was set up. The room was nothing to get excited about, although it was thankfully free of elk decor. Instead, there were prints of ducks on the wall. Jennifer stared at the faded pink and baby blue duck prints for a moment, not sure if they were really an improvement over elk or not. The threadbare carpet was brown and suspiciously stained a darker brown in a couple of places. The queen-sized bed was just a bed and that was the best that could be said about it.

Overall, it was a place to sleep.

Livin' the life.

Somehow, when she'd been working her way through college for a *second* time, this hadn't exactly been what she thought she'd get as her prize at the end. On the other hand, there were a lot of aspects of her life that had turned out wonderfully, so she shouldn't complain too much.

Just because she shouldn't didn't mean she didn't want to, though...

With a groan, she kicked off her conservative pumps and plopped down on the bed. Now that she'd gotten checked in, she needed to find a place to eat and then call Bonnie and commiserate. Bonnie's job was just as awful as hers, so they had lots to commiserate about.

And really, what were best friends for?

Jennifer grabbed her phone and swiped to open so she could do a Google search for a restaurant, when iMessages opened instead, Paul's message in front of her, demanding to be taken care of.

She wrinkled her nose in disgust. She'd been happy to forget all about the text message and live in ignorance, thankyouverymuch, but now that it was open, she ought to just deal with it and move on. Her eyes flicked down the long message once, twice, and then she started at the top again, reading more slowly this time. *Surely this isn't right...*

I know this is hard for u Im sorry ur so confused about what happened Im willing to giv u a second chance to work this out U have to understand that as a dr i have to work closely with nurses other doctors & patients that r female. Ur jealousie is a prob but im willing to let you come back as long as ur working to control that jealousie.

He was willing to forgive *her*?!

Her thumbs hovered over the messaging app as she debated what to say, finally typing, "You're drunk. Stop texting me," and hit send.

It was pretty damn early to be that drunk, but on the other hand, this was Paul. He'd probably been dumped by yet another woman, and had started to make the rounds on his ex's, hoping to find someone who would take him back.

He was nothing if not consistent, considering this was his third attempt at this game. Maybe he thought the third time really was a charm?

Happy to concentrate on something else, she closed the messaging app and switched over to Google Maps. She found a Betty's Diner listed as being on Main Street, which meant she drove right past it on her way in. Whoops. Well, this would give her a chance to go admire Sawyer's Main Street again. She grabbed her wallet, keys, and cell phone, and headed out to her car. Hmmm…food, wine, and *then* she could call Bonnie.

Order of operations. It was a thing.

She headed back down Main Street, this time

focused on the names of the businesses instead of being overwhelmed by their overall cuteness, when she spotted the sign. *Betty's Diner*, with an electronically waving woman in an apron clutching a wooden spoon. How had she missed this on the way in? She must've been sidetracked by the bakery just down the street – The Muffin Man. She'd have to be sure to check that one out, too.

She pulled up into a parking spot in front of Betty's Diner just as her stomach gurgled loudly. The OPEN sign was off, though, and the lights were too. Jennifer got out and walked up to the front door to stare forlornly at the business hours listed there. Open until two o'clock every afternoon.

Two? What kind of restaurant closes at two?!

Stomach still rumbling loudly, Jennifer climbed into her Honda and did another Google search, this time with urgency tingeing her movements. Surely there was another restaurant in town. Surely…

Nothing.

She drove back to the Drop-Inn, this time looking at the town with fewer stars in her eyes. Somehow, she'd found herself at the ass-end of the earth, where restaurants weren't even civilized enough to stay open past mid-afternoon. What did people do around here – eat dinner at home every single night? Wasn't that a little…old-fashioned? Who had time to cook every day, day in and day out?

She pulled up in front of the motel's lobby and got

out, stomping over to the front door with a little less cheer in her step than she'd had before, and woke the blue-haired lady up with an emphatic ring of the bell on the counter. Margaret moseyed on over to the front desk with a cheerful smile, leaving Wheel of Fortune on full blast behind her.

"Yes, dear?" she asked, blinking owlishly at Jenn.

"Do you have the take-out menus for the restaurants here in town?" Jennifer asked, a little desperate at this point. Maybe there was a side street she hadn't driven down, and a wonderful restaurant would be located there, and it would be open, and for whatever reason, they had simply never registered themselves anywhere online.

That was *totally* possible.

"Take-out menus?" Margaret blinked again, obviously struggling to comprehend the question. "Betty's is the best place in town for breakfast and lunch. I don't know anything about their menus being taken out the front door. *I've* certainly never stolen one. But past two o'clock, you have to drive to Franklin."

"How far is that?" she asked, choosing to ignore the "stealing" comment. She had food to find, dammit.

"'Bout thirty minutes away. Opposite direction from Boise."

Which would explain why Jennifer hadn't spotted it on the way to Sawyer this morning. She checked her phone. It was edging towards 7 p.m. She hadn't planned on having to commute an hour round-trip just to find food.

"Is there *any* other place around here that sells food?" she asked, a note of desperation in her voice.

"Well…" the older lady said thoughtfully, "O'Malley's Bar serves dinner. But only during the fair each year, and that ain't until next month. You should come back for it. It's the second weekend of August every year." She paused, waiting for a response, and Jennifer forced a smile onto her face, her hands balling into fists at her sides. She could tell she was on the verge of hangry, which meant it was about to get ugly. "Oh! There's the Muffin Man," Margaret finally continued when Jennifer said nothing. "But it's just donuts and cakes and it closes at five, so Gage has gone home now. You probably shouldn't go to his house and ask him to make you food."

Jennifer just stared at the woman.

I. Will. Kill. You.

"I guess you could probably find something over at Frank's!" she finished triumphantly, excited to suggest something that was actually open. "It's on the main road outta town towards Franklin. On the left. Can't miss it."

"Thanks," Jennifer ground out, and practically ran out of the motel office before she found herself spending the night behind bars for homicide.

Turned out, Frank's was not gourmet food, unless you happened to be a horse. The full name of the business was actually "Frank's Feed & Fuel," where they sold bags of alfalfa pellets next to bags of potato chips. Jennifer settled on a thing called a "tortaco," a fun-sized bag of tortilla chips, and a bottle of generic-brand orange juice.

Returning to her room, she didn't even try to lie to herself about dinner. There was no way to get excited about a tortaco – whatever the hell that was, and especially not one that looked old enough to vote – and there was certainly nothing *fun* about the fun-sized bag of greasy chips.

She sank down on the bed, kicking off her heels again, when she realized a major flaw in her shopping trip: She hadn't managed to get a hold of a bottle of wine anywhere along the way.

Well, she was just too damn tired to go out looking for one now. She'd have to search for a liquor store tomorrow. *If* the ass-end of the earth had such a thing. She was starting to doubt that it did.

Optimism. It was also a thing. Just not a right-now thing.

As she crunched into the tortaco, she looked over at her phone, exhaustion seeping out of every pore. She'd call Bonnie tomorrow. Although friends were there to listen and commiserate, there was only so much complaining someone should have to listen to, and Jennifer was pretty sure that tonight, she'd be serving up an overly large portion.

She'd call her bestie tomorrow, when she could be more positive. No reason to ruin Bonnie's night, too.

With that, she flicked on the grainy TV and settled back to watch reruns of *Home Improvement* and eat greasy chips.

Yup, living the life.

CHAPTER 9

JENNIFER

*A*t 6:30 A.M., the alarm on her phone went off, and Jennifer blearily beat it into submission. No one should have to be awake at this time of day – it should be positively unlawful, actually – but she managed to push herself out of bed anyway. She wasn't about to give Mr. Miller a reason to make another snarky comment by being late to work. She'd get out to the Miller farm at 8 o'clock on the dot if it killed her.

As she studied the motel room's coffee pot, flicking the power switch off and on forlornly, it finally penetrated her non-caffeinated brain that it was totally refusing to turn on or do anything even *remotely* useful – like, say, make coffee.

Getting to work on time just might kill her after all.

After a hot shower, she felt slightly better about the world – although things were relative at this point

– and got dressed. She pulled on her standard audit outfit: A black pencil skirt, black shirt, and black heels. It was hard enough to have farmers take her seriously; dressing the part could only help. It was a little on the severe side, but hey, at least it was professional.

She headed out the door, patting herself on the back for still being on time, despite the lack of caffeine, when she saw the rain that was pelting down. *Dammit.* Her mind flashed back to the long gravel "driveway" out to the Miller farm, and gulped. Hard. She drove a Honda Civic, not a Jeep 4x4.

Tossing her laptop bag into the passenger seat, she headed straight for the farm, deciding to forgo her planned stop for coffee at the Muffin Man. With muddy roads, she'd have to take it slow, and coffee just wasn't meant to be. She could totally live without it for one day.

Maybe.

The rain started coming down harder, and Jennifer slowed down even more, inching along as she switched her wipers into top speed, hunching forward and peering through the front windshield. She was gripping the steering wheel for all she was worth, praying that she wouldn't end up in the ditch on the way out to the farm. That's all this audit needed – her car having to be towed out of a ditch.

Cursing a blue streak, she pulled up in front of the Miller farmhouse, the clock on her dashboard blinking 8:09. She was late. If it wasn't for the rain…

But as Greg always said, people wanted results,

not excuses. And this morning, all she had was excuses.

She peered through the sheets of rain coming down to spot Mr. Miller on the covered front porch, watching her, coffee cup in hand. *Dammmmmmiiittttttt.* She'd been hoping she'd be able to sneak inside and he wouldn't notice her tardiness.

Well, no hope for that now. With a huge sigh, she grabbed her laptop bag and swung out of the Honda, planting her feet firmly in a giant puddle, water splashing up her legs and filling up the soles of her high heels.

Of *course* it did.

She wanted nothing more in that moment than to swing her feet back inside the car, put it in drive, and go back to Boise. Forget this whole thing had ever happened.

Hmmmm…scratch that. She wanted coffee *slightly* more than that.

Which…Carmelita was her closest source of the stuff, dammit all, so if for no other reason than the pursuit of caffeine, Jennifer made herself get out of her car, sling her bag over her shoulder, and stride up to the front porch as if nothing were wrong. As if her shoes weren't squelching with water and mud with every step, with more rain pouring down on her as she went.

Under the cover of the porch stood a dry and smirking Mr. Miller, holding his coffee cup that proudly proclaimed "This Ain't My First Rodeo" in one hand, while holding his other arm up in front of his face to ostentatiously check his watch.

"You *almost* made it," he said as he lowered the cup. Was there a hint of...amusement in his voice? He was probably laughing at her stepping into a puddle so large, the federal government was – at this very moment – making plans to put it into new maps for the area as a place to go fishing.

"Yeah, well, I tried," Jennifer grumbled as she clomped up the porch steps. She shifted from foot to foot, miserable and cold and wet. This was *not* how she'd envisioned the morning going.

He shrugged. "This place isn't exactly built for Honda Civics. I suppose I can overlook it just this once."

Jennifer swallowed hard – he was trying to be nice, but on the other hand, she didn't really appreciate his condescending attitude in deigning to overlook her faults just this one time.

She swallowed her pride, nodded her acceptance, and headed inside, kicking her high heels off at the front door. She was pretty sure Carmelita wouldn't want her tracking mud through the house, although her pantyhose was only marginally cleaner than her shoes.

Speaking of... Carmelita came bustling in, and with one look at her sodden appearance, clucked her tongue in sympathy. "Let me find a towel for you. Do not move."

She headed back into the bowels of the house,

talking to herself as she went, as Mr. Miller came inside. Trying to get out of the way, Jennifer stepped to the side, but she misjudged which direction he was going and they collided instead. Jennifer flushed a deep red as she tried to scurry out of his way yet again. He stood there for a moment, just staring at her, and she finally burst out, "What?! I'll get to the audit in just a minute, I promise. I know I'm late. Carmelita wants me to wait—"

"No, it isn't that," he interrupted, holding up a hand and stopping her. "It's just that I want to get to the coat closet behind you." He pointed over her shoulder at the alcove of coats that she'd been inadvertently guarding.

"Oh. Right." She sent him a weak smile as she moved out of his way yet again.

This was going to be the longest two weeks of her life, no doubt about it.

CHAPTER 10

STETSON

So, he was kinda an asshole.

He knew it, and wasn't surprised by it. He owned that title and ran with it...most of the time.

He'd intentionally taken his coffee outside that morning, ostensibly to enjoy the patter of rain on the covered porch and look out over his family's farm, but in reality, because he wanted to see if the thief really would show up on time. He wanted to rub it in her face when she didn't.

And even though she had been late, when she'd stepped out of her car and right into that giant puddle, he'd been entertained instead of pissed. He should've been mad that she was wasting time – not treating his case with the respect that it deserved. Instead...

Well, it was hard to be mad at a drowned rat, and especially a drowned rat in a very nice skirt.

Muttering curses he didn't dare say within Carmelita's hearing, Stetson headed to the barn. The hired hands had vaccinated the calves yesterday under the direction of Christian, everyone was fed, and with this rain pouring down, it wasn't a terrific day to be outside anyway. He needed to replace that section of fence out in the triangle pasture before some cow figured out that she could push her way through, but...

Not today.

He found himself in front of Grandpa's tractor, staring at it contemplatively. If he just did a full tune-up and replaced the valve cover gaskets, he could probably have it running by the end of the day. He looked at the tires, worn and beat up, but still holding together. They could probably stand to be replaced, but who had money to spend on nostalgia? He'd make do with the old tires for a while. See what happened with this audit, then decide.

The audit...

Stetson wrenched at a bolt a little too hard, the screech of abused, rusty metal giving way echoing in the barn's rafters, but he couldn't make himself care. No matter how cute the thief was and how adorable she looked, her soaked hair hanging in her eyes, she was still the enemy, and he would do well to remember that.

CHAPTER 11

JENNIFER

SHE POURED OVER the documents in front of her, trying to piece the complex business together. Mr. Miller seemed to be quite unusual compared to the other farmers that Intermountain Bank lent to, in that he didn't seem to focus on one or two crops or animals, but rather was doing All of the Above.

Hay, cows, corn, wheat...most farmers were monolithic in their approach to farming, choosing to do one or two things really, really well, rather than trying to do a lot of things mostly well. It meant the risks were higher – if it was a bad potato year and that's all the farmer had planted, well, they were shit out of luck – but it was also easier to maintain and keep up on. Less specialized machinery, less moving parts to keep track of, less complexity overall.

Which made Mr. Miller's choice to do it all fairly unusual.

She wondered for a moment why Mr. Miller was choosing this particular path to go down, and even contemplated finding him to ask him just that, when she heard a soft knock at the office door. She stood up and turned around rather than risk trying to rotate in the Fainting Goat Chair – as she'd come to call it in her mind – when she saw Carmelita at the door.

"I thought you could use some coffee," she said in her light Hispanic accent, holding a rose-patterned mug out to Jennifer.

"Oh yes, please!" Jennifer said delightedly, taking the cup into her hands and breathing in deep. "Thank you. The coffeemaker was broken in the motel room this morning, so I honestly haven't been able to properly wake up yet." She took a deep sip of the rich, dark brown ambrosia and heaved a sigh of pure pleasure.

"Did you eat breakfast?" the housekeeper asked, her brow wrinkling with worry. "You are too skinny – you must eat more."

As if on cue, her stomach let out a loud rumble. Jennifer didn't tend to eat a lot in the mornings, but dinner last night had left a lot to be desired, and apparently, her stomach was in full revolt over that fact. She grimaced and Carmelita laughed.

"You come eat. I will make you breakfast." She turned and headed back down the hallway without waiting for a response. Jennifer hurried after her, coffee cup in hand.

"But Mr. Miller will be upset," she protested, even

as her stomach let out another rumble. *Shut up.* It was *not* helping matters. "He said lunch only."

"My Stetson does not tell me who I will feed in my kitchen," the housekeeper said as they got to the kitchen and she began pulling out bowls and ingredients, setting to work on making enough food for a small army. "If he wants me to cook for him, then he will allow me to cook for others, too. He likes my tamales too much to tell me no." She winked at Jennifer as she put some sausages in the pan to fry.

Jennifer laughed a little at that, taking another sip of her coffee as she tried to wake up. "How long have you worked for the Millers?"

"Oh, too many years to count," Carmelita said with a laugh. "Stetson's grandfather hired me when I was just a girl – only 19 – and I have been here ever since. The boys joke that I am an inheritance – passed down from father to son – but then I tell them that I am the best thing they could inherit." She chuckled. "Stetson was only a boy when his momma died, so I love him the most, but do not tell the others I said that. Like a good mother hen, I must pretend I love them all equally."

Jennifer let out a bark of laughter at that, and then a sigh of joy when Carmelita slid a plate of waffles, eggs, and sausage in front of her. It looked like enough food for breakfast, lunch, and dinner, but she doubted Carmelita would listen to her protests, so she just dug in instead. "How old was Stetson when Mrs. Miller passed away?"

"Only twelve. Just a baby, really. Wyatt had already left the house and Declan, too. It was just Stetson's mom, dad, Stetson, and me here. To lose Mrs. Miller…it was very hard for everyone."

Jennifer nodded slowly, trying to wrap her mind around the idea of a skinny, pre-teen fumbling around, a little lost in the world and not sure where to turn to. His anger began to make sense, even if Jennifer didn't appreciate it being directed at her.

"So, do you have any family of your own?" Jennifer asked, wanting to change the subject. Contemplating a prepubescent boy without a mother made Mr. Miller too likable. Too human. It was easier to keep him at a distance instead.

Carmelita laughed and shook her head. "I have a few sisters but they are married with children of their own. I had a man propose once, but I did not want to leave the Miller Farm, and he would not move here. So, it was not meant to be." She shrugged practically as she cleaned up from breakfast. "I am not so sad about this. The Millers are my family in my heart. I just wish that…"

"Wish what?" Mr. Miller asked in his deep voice, and Jennifer froze. She hadn't heard him coming in. How had she missed his cowboy boots on the hardwood floors? She whipped around in her chair and stared up at him, her fork still on its way to her mouth. Realizing how ridiculous she looked, she quickly put it down, wanting to follow it and hide underneath the table.

Maybe Carmelita was okay with breaking his rules, but Jennifer wasn't so sure she was.

"That all of my boys could get along," Carmelita said, staring him in the eye as she did so.

Jennifer had to give her kudos – she had one hell of a backbone. A muscle twitched in Mr. Miller's jaw but Carmelita didn't seem to notice, or more to the point, didn't seem to care. She simply stared back evenly, the ticking of the clock on the wall the only sound.

Now she *really* wanted to hide under the table. Family drama…this was *not* what Jennifer had signed up for. Balance bank statements. Track funding. Figure out if there was anything that could be sold to pay the debt to the bank. *That* was her job.

This…this was *way* outside of her comfort zone.

"I will get along with Wyatt," Mr. Miller growled, "as soon as he quits blaming the world for his wife and child's death. Until then, I can't help him."

He turned on his heel and headed out the front door, the windows rattling as he slammed it shut behind him. Carmelita turned back towards Jennifer, tutting as she did. "Sometimes, it is possible to be right and wrong at the same time. My Stetson is very good at that. Here, let me clean up your plate, and then I must go to the store. I do not like to drive in the rain, but I am almost out of chiles and you cannot make salsa without chiles."

Apparently unfazed by Mr. Miller's anger, the housekeeper took Jennifer's plate – which Jennifer realized with a start was pretty much cleaned off; she must've been hungrier than she realized – and turned to the sink to wash up.

Jennifer grabbed her mug of coffee and headed back down to the office to get back to work. Maybe the housekeeper wasn't intimidated by an overgrown, angry-at-everyone-and-everything Mr. Miller, but Jenn was. He could be angry at the world without her having to be a part of it.

The sooner she could finish this audit and get out of here, the better.

CHAPTER 12

STETSON

S TETSON STORMED back to the barn, cursing with every step. First, he'd realized that he'd forgotten to bring rags out to the barn that morning to refill his stockpile, and then when he went inside to grab some, he'd caught Carmelita telling that banker all about the Miller family history, and then he'd stormed back outside…without any rags.

He was back where he started, having accomplished nothing but getting pissy at the world. Which he wouldn't exactly consider to be progress.

He grabbed a 3/4-inch wrench and set about removing the tractor weights off his grandfather's tractor so he could get to the engine. He would restore the antique and then he would tell Jennifer the Thief to leave his farm and then he would wake up and realize that this was all a bad dream.

That totally seemed like a valid plan. He especially liked the part where he woke up to find it was a bad dream. He'd been trying to implement that part of the plan for months now, but it never did seem to actually happen.

Which really was too damn bad.

"I...will not...let some female...steal my...farm!" he shouted between grunts as he pushed on the wrench. "She can just...go back...to Boise! I–*argh!*" His hand slipped off the wrench and smashed against the grille of the tractor, slicing his knuckles open. "Shit!" he bellowed, dropping the wrench and clasping his bloody hand against his chest. He grabbed the last mostly clean rag off the bench and wrapped it around his hand, watching as it turned a brilliant red within moments. "Dammit, dammit, dammit!" he hollered.

Just what he needed – an ER bill on top of everything else.

He slogged back through the mud and rain towards the house as quickly as he could. If he could get Carmelita to clean the wound and bandage it up tight, he could avoid a huge medical bill. Maybe.

He could always hope, although he'd be the first one to admit that luck hadn't exactly been on his side lately.

CHAPTER 13

JENNIFER

*W*ITH A SIGH, Jennifer pulled another drawer open. It seemed like they were endless, even though she knew intellectually that she'd made it through half of them. It just didn't feel like it. Because of how many different projects were being tackled here on the farm, this had to be the most complex audit Jennifer had ever been assigned, which Greg was *not* going to be happy about. He wanted answers...

Oh shit! Jennifer jumped up, rummaging through her laptop bag quickly, trying to find her phone. Dammit, dammit. She was supposed to call him at noon today to give an update, and it was now...she looked up at the bugling elk up on the wall...after two. As if he needed an excuse to be pissed off.

She finally latched onto her phone – buried in the bottom, like always – and hurried out into the hallway. She had to go outside and stand on the front porch to get enough reception to talk to Greg, but at least it was an enclosed porch so she wouldn't have to get soaked while doing it. She wasn't sure if she could endure that insult to injury. She'd barely dried all the way through from her dousing that morning.

Just as she got to the end of the hallway, the front door opened and Mr. Miller came through, bellowing at the top of his lungs, "Carmelita! Where's the damn first aid kit?"

He was clutching his right hand, a dark and bloodied rag wrapped around it. "She's gone to the store," Jennifer gasped, even as she was hurrying to his side, dropping her phone on the entryway table as she went. "What happened?" She took his hand into hers, peeling the rag away and watching the knuckles refill with blood.

"Tractor. It got me."

She tugged him towards the kitchen. "C'mon, let's get you over the sink before you drip blood everywhere. Something tells me that Carmelita wouldn't appreciate coming home to that."

He chuckled and followed her obediently. "You know her already," he said dryly as he held his hand over the sink.

She looked up at him and grinned. "She's not that hard to figure out. I'm not sure if she cleans the house so much as just terrifies the dust to the point that it wouldn't dare to stray in here." He let out a loud laugh at that, his straight white teeth flashing against his chiseled jaw. She swallowed hard. *Focus, Jennifer.*

"Now, where would the bandages be? The bathroom? The pantry?"

"The pantry? I think?"

He's such a guy sometimes. She rolled her eyes to herself. If Carmelita wasn't here to keep him in line, the whole house would be as disastrous as his office. And that was *not* a pretty thing to contemplate.

She was heading for the walk-in pantry at the end of the kitchen counter to start the search there when he hollered, "Hold on! Why are *you* helping me?" It was as if the situation had just registered in his mind.

She ignored the question until she found the white box, a giant red cross on the front, and emerged from the oversized closet triumphantly. "I used to be a nurse," she said with a shrug. "It's been a while, but I'm pretty sure I remember how to bandage a hand."

"Nurse to banker, huh?"

She turned on the cold water and ran it over his hand, trying to irrigate the wound. His slight intake of breath was the only indication that it hurt. *Well, at least he isn't a whiner.*

"Accountant," she corrected him. "I ended up at the Intermountain Bank because they were the only ones hiring when I graduated, and I have a *lot* of student loans to pay off. College is expensive enough, without going through it twice."

She shut up. He didn't want to hear her whine and complain about money. If she couldn't find a way to help him, he'd lose the family farm.

Which suddenly seemed like a much bigger deal

than a few student loans, even if her debt was in the high five figures. There was a difference; even she could see that.

"What made you switch careers?" he asked as she rummaged through the kit, looking for gauze and an ace wrap.

She paused for just a moment in her hunt, trying to decide what to tell him, and then said lightly, "A guy. We...had a difference of opinion. He thought it was okay to cheat on me; I didn't happen to agree." She shot him an overly bright smile and began gently placing the gauze over the wound and then wrapping it up. "He was a doctor. I'd worked as a low-level nurse for years to put him through medical school, and when he graduated, he was supposed to work as a doctor to bring in income while I became an RN. I fulfilled my part of the bargain. I can't say he did the same in return."

She looked up at Stetso—Mr. Miller with a fake smile. "It's in the past. I don't think about it much anymore." *Except when he starts texting me out of the blue and telling me that he's willing to forgive me.*

She kept that part to herself.

She looked down at the bandaged hand with a critical eye. *Hmmmm....Not bad after taking a couple of years off.*

She looked up and realized that he too had been studying his hand and now their faces were close together and her heart was knocking against her ribcage and his eyes were flicking down towards her lips and she stopped breathing and...

Gravel crunched outside, then the garage door opened with a creak and a groan. They sprung apart from each other, and Jennifer looked around the kitchen frantically. "I need to call my boss," she announced, searching for her phone. Where had she put it down?

Oh. Right. Out in the hallway. Where I saw Stetso—Mr. Miller come in from outside.

"I better go find my phone, Mr. Miller. My boss was expecting a phone call a couple of hours ago."

"Stetson. Mr. Miller is my father."

She bit her lip, staring up at him – wayyyyy up at him since she hadn't put her heels back on – and nodded. Once. "Stetson," she said softly, and then ran out of the kitchen.

She needed to call her boss, and she needed to stop drooling over handsome cowboys.

She wasn't sure which task was going to be harder.

CHAPTER 14

STETSON

*A*FTER HE HELPED Carmelita bring the groceries in from the car and let her cluck and worry over his hand, Stetson headed out the back door and down the best sledding slope in the county during the winter. Since it was most assuredly *not* winter, the hill currently was slippery and muddy and nasty, but he headed down it anyway. He'd hidden away in the barn for long enough. It was time to go check fences and make sure that his cows were where they were supposed to be. He could only ignore that for so long, no matter how miserable it was to be out in a rainstorm.

He got to the storage shed at the base of the hill and backed his four-wheeler out. As much as his friend Adam would hate to admit it, a four-wheeler was a farmer's best friend, not a horse. A four-wheeler didn't need to be fed or vaccinated or taken out for rides. It didn't get lonely or break a leg in a hole, and it sure as shit didn't get sick from being fed something less than premium hay.

He started down his fence lines, getting off occasionally to open and close gates along the way, checking to make sure that the cows were where they were supposed to be, and the fences were where they were supposed to be, and the torrential rains hadn't rearranged something important.

The cows were huddled together in groups, miserable and wet in the pouring rain, but at least they weren't busy trying to push fences over. That was always a plus.

As Stetson continued into another pasture, the cold rain dripping down off his hat and down the collar of his jacket while the movement of the four-wheeler jostled his wounded hand, he forced himself to focus on that pain. If he focused on it, then maybe he wouldn't think about the bright green eyes of an accountant, peering up at him over his bandaged hand.

Anything to keep from thinking about that.

*A*FTER QUIZZING the housekeeper on the best place to find food in town after two o'clock, Jennifer headed back to town with a happy sigh. All in all, not a bad day. She'd made it through the filing cabinets, matching expenses with the withdrawals from the checking account.

Soon, she'd be tackling the truly important part: Finding assets to sell. If she could find something – preferably multiple somethings – to sell, then Stetson could make his yearly payment to the bank, and at least muddle his way through another year. Maybe with another year to right his ship, he could be back to making the yearly payments that the Miller family had never missed up to this point.

Jennifer pulled up in front of the Shop 'N Go grocery store and saw that it was open until nine at night. Why hadn't Margaret directed her towards this place last night instead of an animal supply store?

With a roll of her eyes at the complete lack of help from the older lady, Jennifer hit the aisles of the store, wandering up and down them with a tiny shopping cart. Even the owners of Shop 'N Go didn't expect her to buy much from their store and one look at the prices told her why. There were artisan specialty stores in Boise with more reasonable prices than the Shop 'N Go had.

But at least she wasn't going to have to eat tortacos tonight, and for that, she was grateful.

She picked out the makings of a salad – greens, shredded cooked chicken, nuts, and dressing – that would be easy to assemble in her motel room, and then made her way over to the wine aisle. Hmmm…not the largest selection in the world, but beggars couldn't be choosers. She finally picked out a white wine in a beautiful blue bottle that made her wish that decorating with empty wine bottles was a "thing," paid the exorbitant bill at the front cash register, and tucked the receipt in her purse for safe keeping. She wasn't sure which was more of a pain in the ass – going through someone else's receipts in an audit, or keeping track of her own receipts to turn in for reimbursement at the end of an audit.

After a mostly satisfying meal and a filling up of a plastic cup from the bathroom sink with wine – she'd forgotten to buy a wine glass while at the Shop 'N Go, if they even carried such a thing – she settled down on the queen bed with a sigh. Finally, she could relax.

She picked up her cell phone and hit Favorite 1 to call Bonnie.

"There you are!" her friend answered with a laugh. "I was starting to think that the good people of Sawyer had kidnapped you and taken your phone away from you."

"Eh, it's just been a busy few days." Filled with mud, and handsome, surly cowboys, and sweet housekeepers. Jennifer was suddenly unsure how much she wanted to tell her best friend.

Which was just weird, because she told Bonnie everything. You don't go through all that she and Bonnie had, and keep secrets from each other afterward.

"Sooooo…" Bonnie said, a teasing tone in her voice, "how handsome is the farmer?"

Jennifer had known the question was coming. It was always Bonnie's first question when Jennifer was doing an audit. It had become a long-standing joke between them, because the answer was always easy to give: *He's 82 years old with more wrinkles than a linen shirt;* or *he's 57 with a pot gut;* or *he and his wife have been married for longer than I've been alive.*

But even though she'd known the question was coming, she still didn't have an answer at the ready. She sat there hesitantly for a minute, until Bonnie bursted out laughing. "Oh! My! God!" she gasped. "You're kidding me. This guy is actually cute? And single?"

"Well, I haven't asked him if he's dating anyone," Jennifer answered weakly.

"Oh Jennifer!" Bonnie shouted, dissolving into laughter again. "You have to tell me all about him. How handsome is he?"

Sexy as sin popped into Jennifer's mind, but she pushed it away. "You know I can't date a client, especially not one that I'm auditing," she protested. "He's just a little more handsome than normal, is all."

"Height," Bonnie said, ignoring her protestations.

"Six-foot-two, maybe? Six-foot-three? I don't know. Even in my heels, he towers over me."

"Hair color." It was an order, not a question. Jennifer thought about protesting again, but gave in, instead. It wasn't because she wanted to talk about Stetson Miller, of course. It was just because she knew how stubborn Bonnie was, and knew that Bonnie would continue to push her if she refused to answer her questions. So it was just easier to give in.

Nothing more than that.

"Dark brown, but sun-bleached up on top. You can tell that he spends a lot of time outside. I bet he has one hell of a farmer's tan."

"And yet, you were trying to give off the impression that you've hardly thought about him at all," Bonnie said dryly.

Jennifer had no ready response for that, so she just took another drink of her wine instead.

"Name?"

"Stetson Miller."

"Stetson? Like the cowboy hat?"

"Yeah."

"Does he wear the Stetson brand?"

"I don't know! I don't pick out his clothes every morning!" Jennifer said, exasperated. "He wears Wranglers, I know that much. I haven't studied the inside of his cowboy hat for brand names."

"And exactly what were you doing to figure out that he wears Wranglers?" Bonnie asked.

"I saw the leather tag on his ass as he walked away—*shit*!" she finished when she realized that she was admitting to staring at her client's ass.

"Fascinating," Bonnie said, and Jennifer stuck her tongue out. Bonnie couldn't see her which rather ruined the effect, but Jennifer couldn't help it.

"Do I like you?" Jennifer grumbled. "I can't remember right now."

"Yup!" Bonnie said cheerfully. "So, are you going to be able to help him save his farm?"

"I don't know," Jennifer said forlornly. "I wish I knew. Because I don't want to have to tell him that the Miller Family Farm that's been in Miller hands since the 1800s is now owned by Intermountain Bank & Loan. That always sucks, but it'd suck especially bad this time. Not only for Stetson, but also his housekeeper. She's been with the family since she was 19. She's never lived anywhere else. They'd be homeless. I can't…I hate my job, you know that? I really damn well hate it."

"I know," Bonnie said quietly, serious for the first

time in the conversation. "I'm not sure I could do what you do."

This job had never been something Jennifer loved with all of her heart and soul, but it was quickly descending into outright hatred and disgust. It was so far removed from what she'd originally set out to do, she felt like a failure.

If she couldn't help Stetson save his farm, she would hate herself even more, and right now, that was really saying something.

CHAPTER 16

STETSON

*H*E WASN'T going to do it. He went to bed the night before, firm in the conviction that he wasn't going to be around when Jennifer-the-Accountant-Definitely-Not-a-Banker-Maybe-a-Thief showed up to work. She knew how to find his farm, so she could get to work without him being there to watch her do it.

But, it was raining again – still? – this morning, having not stopped since the first drops began to fall early yesterday morning, so the mud was getting deeper and the gravel was getting more treacherous. She did drive a little Civic; it was possible that her car wouldn't make it from town to farm without sliding into the borrow pit somewhere along the way. He should make sure that she made it to the farm safely before getting to work for the day. Right?

Why? So you can be sure that she makes it safely to your

father's office and gets right to work stealing your family's farm away from you?

He grunted in frustration. No, his first instinct was absolutely correct. He shouldn't be anywhere near the farmhouse when little Miss Boise showed up in her little Honda Civic car and her high heels and her skirts to invade his father's office once again.

Absolutely not.

Which was why it was a surprise to no one at all, least of all Stetson, when he found himself on the long covered porch at 7:57 a.m., watching Jennifer pull up. Today's coffee cup read, "You say 'Raised in a barn' like it's a bad thing," which seemed even more appropriate than usual.

He watched as she carefully navigated around the large puddle that had been her nemesis the day before until she found a dry spot – relatively speaking, of course – to park. She got out and walked around the car, slinging her laptop bag over her shoulder as she went, and Stetson's eyes followed her every movement, sweeping down her slim body, mouth going dry as he stared at her legs beneath the swish of her skirt.

Unbidden, he opened the front door for her, no sarcastic remark to make today. She was on time, and they both knew it. She sent him a flustered smile as she passed, probably trying to figure out what his angle was.

He left her to walk inside by herself, not following

behind her so he could continue admiring her ass and legs, but instead forcing himself to do what he should've done earlier: Get to work. He still had more fence to ride, even if it was pouring down rain – maybe especially because it was pouring down rain – and staring at the legs and ass of the accountant here to steal his farm away from him wasn't going to be how that happened.

He forced himself to put his coffee cup down on the porch railing, walk down the front steps, and head for the storage shed again to retrieve his four-wheeler.

He was a farmer, and farmers worked. They did not drool. Not even over the finest legs God ever did send to the earth.

CHAPTER 17

JENNIFER

*J*ENNIFER SETTLED down in the Fainting Goat Chair and stared at the piles in front of her. She had gone through the costs of running the Miller Family Farm, and now was the time to start into the income pile. Not surprisingly, this pile of receipts was much smaller. Wasn't that always how it went?

Hmmm…she picked up a paid invoice for one of the swankiest restaurants in Boise. She looked at the bottom line of the invoice and let out a low whistle. Stetson had to be raising some pretty high-end cows if he was selling them at *this* price.

"What?" he asked, his deep voice startling her out of her thoughts.

And out of her chair. With a yelp, she tried to spin in the chair towards the office door but instead she found herself on the floor, staring at the ceiling.

Again.

He hurried to her side and helped her onto her feet as she brushed at her clothing.

Again.

"That chair is...temperamental," Stetson said in way of apology as he stood back and let her try to straighten herself out. "My dad kept saying he was going to get a new chair someday, but he never did, and...well, I didn't either." He didn't say anything else, and Jennifer wondered where that thought would've ended if he considered her to be a friend and someone he could talk to. She was pretty sure that there was more there than he was offering up.

"I'm usually more careful in the Fainting Goat Chair, but you startled me," she admitted with a little laugh, looking up, up, up at him.

He really should stop eating Wheaties in the morning. She was pretty sure he'd already grown all that he should by this point.

"Fainting Goat—" Stetson said with a startled snort of a laugh. "You know, that's just about the perfect name for it."

They stopped and stared at each other for a minute. Jennifer was getting a crick in her neck, and had to keep herself from putting her high heels on and then continuing to talk to him. Or insisting that he sit in the chair.

But she wasn't about to admit weakness.

Never admit weakness.

"So why were you whistling?" Stetson asked, his dark brown eyes ensnaring hers. Trapping her.

Making her feel like the most important person he'd ever talked to. Jennifer had the fleeting question of whether everyone felt that way around Stetson, and then dismissed the thought. She needed to concentrate.

"Your cows," she forced herself to say, focusing on his question. "That's a damn fine price per pound that you're selling at, especially on the hoof. Is the restaurant taking care of the butchering step?"

He nodded. "They have a specialty butcher who hangs and cures and does everything the way the restaurant wants. A typical butcher wouldn't be able to get it just right for them. There's a reason why a T-bone steak is so damn expensive there."

"I...I don't get it," Jennifer admitted, and then swallowed hard.

Saying something like that out loud – especially to *Stetson* of all people – burned her biscuit. Truth was, though, she was totally stumped and out of options. She had to ask questions because going in circles while staring at the books was doing her no good at all.

She cleared her throat and plunged on. "I've seen your costs. I've seen your expenses. I've seen some of your income – I just got started on that part today, I'll admit. But I see how you live. You *should* be able to make the yearly payment to the bank without breaking a sweat. But you have these huge transfers to your personal account, way more than your lifestyle here would demand. Do you have a bevy of prostitutes or mistresses tucked away somewhere, that you're keeping in style?"

"A bevy of..." Stetson let out another snort of laughter. "I don't have a bevy of prostitutes or mistresses or anyone else hidden away. Is that a typical expense that you find while auditing books?"

She glared up at him. He was laughing at her, and she wasn't quite sure she appreciated that. "So, if it isn't prostitutes or mistresses, what is it? A gambling problem?"

"Gambling...good Lord. You have a real high opinion of me, don't you?"

This time, she added crossed arms to the glare. "I just met you three days ago. I don't think I could have formed an opinion of you – good *or* bad – by this point." Well, she had – that he was an overgrown ape with the manners of a caveman – but she wasn't about to tell him that. She wasn't going to let him score a point, even if it meant losing out on the chance to insult him.

Which really was too bad, honestly.

"My dad," he said simply, and then shrugged.

She stared. He stared back. The clock ticked on the wall. A cow lowed in the distance.

"Your dad what?" Jennifer asked, breaking first. She hated giving in and actually asking him what he meant by his purposefully obtuse statement, but she also hated not knowing.

It was quite the predicament to be in.

"His cancer treatments," Stetson said simply, as if

it were obvious. "That's what I spent all of the money on. The cows made me enough money to pay for his cancer treatments. My wheat, corn, and hay made me enough money to pay Carmelita, Christian, and my other employees, and cover the costs of my living expenses, scarce as they are, but that's all the crops I raise. There was no crop left to sell that would bring in money to pay the bank."

"Oh." She blinked, her frustration with him slowly deflating as she put it together. *Jennifer, you really stepped in it this time.* "How long did your father have cancer?" she asked softly.

"Eighteen months. After the first round of chemo, he didn't want to fight it anymore, but I...I pushed him." His voice went flat and quiet, and his gaze skittered away from hers. "I wasn't ready to lose him yet. I talked him into another round, and...I shouldn't have. It was selfish of me. He was in a lot of pain."

He was staring at the far wall over her shoulder as he talked, and she swallowed. Hard. She officially felt like an ass, which wasn't exactly a pleasant feeling.

"So why all of the crops?" she asked, hoping to steer the conversation towards something less painful, which would include almost every topic on the planet at this point.

"Why all of what crops?" he repeated, confused. He was looking at her again, and she suddenly found herself wishing that he'd go back to staring at the wall. He was entirely too handsome for his own good.

Or hers.

"Usually, a rancher raises cows, or a farmer does hay or corn or potatoes or whatever. You do everything. It's…unusual. I've been wondering about that for a couple of days now."

"Honestly, I shouldn't." He shrugged. "Millers are row croppers. Beets, corn, whatever. If it grows in a straight line, that's our cup of tea. I had a brilliant idea when I was a kid that I wanted to do cows. Wheat was boring, you know? Row after row, field after field…it wasn't where my heart was. So when I was 17, I finally talked my dad into letting me buy a small herd of cows. He thought I'd lost my ever-lovin' mind, but he let me do it anyway. I think he expected me to fail and get it out of my system and then go back to doing what Millers were *supposed* to do."

He smiled a little, just a small twist of the lips. "Instead, I slowly grew the herd over time, and found a Boise restaurant to sell organic, specialty beef to, and then another restaurant, and…here we are. If Dad had gotten cancer a couple of years later, or if I hadn't insisted that we do an extra round of treatment, I probably could've made my payment to the bank this year." He shrugged again. "Live and learn, I suppose."

His dark brown eyes were hooded with pain and Jennifer reached up without thinking about it to stroke his cheek. She shouldn't have because he was a client and she was an employee of the bank and no matter how much she wanted to, she couldn't forget that she may have to recommend foreclosure some day in the future, but none of that mattered in that moment, and her fingers touched his stubbled cheek anyway.

As soon as they did, her breath stopped and she stared, her body on fire from the touch and him and he stared back, unblinking...

And then he was gone, his boots echoing down the hallway as he hurried out of the house and away from her.

Away from the person who was probably going to have to ruin his life.

And she didn't blame him one bit for running.

CHAPTER 18

STETSON

*H*E WAS an *idiot*. There was no reason for him to tell her everything that he just did. Why did he say it? What was he thinking? She'd been standing there, so small and petite, her huge brilliant green eyes swallowing up her face as she'd bit her lip and looked up at him, and he'd felt, for a moment, that he could trust her. That she was on his team.

Which was ridiculous. She worked for the bank. She was here to steal his farm away.

Her soulful eyes burned through his memories, and he asked himself the question he hadn't dared to allow himself to ask before – was he *sure* about that? If she really was here to steal his farm away, she sure was doing a bang-up job of pretending to care.

Of course, this had happened before. Not the part about the banker trying to steal his farm, of course, but the part where the woman pretended to care. All the way up until she didn't show up at the altar.

That was a hell of a snow job. He still had no idea why Michelle did what she did. What had she been hoping to get out of it?

He figured he'd go to his grave, wondering that.

He looked around, realizing that he'd somehow ended up back in the barn, standing in front of Grandpa's tractor again. Maybe some small part of his psyche knew that he should fix it so he could move on with his life. Maybe it was some sort of metaphor that only his subconscious understood.

He'd gone into the house to grab his rain slicker so he could do some repair work on a fence, which didn't explain why he'd gone past the coat alcove and to the door of the office to retrieve it, considering it was in fact in the coat alcove, not the office.

He'd told himself that he just wanted to check up on her; see how she was doing. See if maybe she was searching through the trash cans after all. She wasn't, dammit all – he could hate her so much easier if she had been – and then she'd let out that low whistle, and he'd had to know.

Well, now he knew: Jennifer knew what the price should be for beef on the hoof – which even he had to admit was impressive – and she had the most gorgeous green eyes he'd ever seen in his life. Like the color of new grass in the spring, pushing up through the mud and the snow to start life anew again.

He wasn't entirely sure which piece of

information was more dangerous, but he did know that combined together, it was a hell of a lethal combination.

And he couldn't say he was exactly thrilled by that realization.

CHAPTER 19

JENNIFER

*J*ENNIFER'S EYES flicked towards the bugling elk on the wall. 4:57…close enough. She'd been a good girl. She'd gotten lots done. She'd sorted through the last of the papers. She'd almost kissed a client.

Hmmm…maybe she'd leave that last part off her report.

She shoved her laptop into her bag and grabbed a stack of papers to work on in the hotel room. She could work on them over dinner, while watching another rerun of *Home Improvement.* Would Wilson show his face on camera today? She should watch, just in case. Cramming the receipts into the pocket of the computer bag, she lifted the strap over her shoulder just as her phone began to buzz with "Working Overtime." *Dammit.* Greg.

At first, the ring tone had been a joke, but now, it was a harbinger of doom. Dinner dates, weekend trips, even movies with friends, all died a swift but painful death when that ring tone played. She had to battle the urge to break her phone every time she heard it, even when it was on the radio.

As she scurried through the house to the front porch, she glanced down and realized that the battery icon was a dangerous red color. She'd forgotten to plug it in the night before after talking to Bonnie for hours, and had meant to plug it in at the Miller house but had forgotten again. *Shit.* Hopefully there was still enough battery left for this phone call. Her job probably wouldn't survive her hanging up on her boss, low battery or not.

She swiped her finger across the screen to answer the call even before she was fully on the porch, dumping her computer bag on a rocking chair. "This is Jennifer Kendall," she got out, trying to hide her breathlessness from her sprint through the house. The pattering of rain on the porch overhang was soothing. The mist drifted towards her and she shivered from the cold. She should put on her jacket, even if it was designed for looks, not warmth. It could only help.

"What the hell takes you so long to answer the damn phone?" Greg snarled, making no attempt to hide his mood.

"The reception is poor here," she said, struggling into the jacket one arm at a time, trying not to drop her phone in the process. She was pretty sure that'd be almost as bad as hanging up on him. "I have to go outside to be able to hear you."

"What have I told you about excuses? Now is *really* not the time. Are you done with the audit yet?"

"Of course I'm not done yet." She tried to keep the frustration out of her voice, but she was pretty sure she was failing. She stared out across the fields, watching the white fence posts march endlessly into the distance. The craggy mountains opposite the farmhouse rose up in the sky, majestic and white-peaked even in July, edging the sides of the wide valley they embraced.

It truly is beautiful out in the country.

"I want this done as quickly as possible. I want options on my desk ASAP," Greg said, pronouncing the acronym as 'A-sap' rather than spelling it out.

"I'm working as fast as I can," Jennifer responded flatly, her attention on the beauty in front of her. Dark rain clouds hung low in the distance. There was a misty, ethereal quality to the farm, like she'd been dropped into another world. She watched as cows wandered along, giving out low, deep *moooo's* to their calves that weren't keeping pace.

"I don't understand what the problem is. Why's this taking so long?" he demanded.

"It's only the third day I've been here, and I'd explain why it's taking so long, but I've already heard your rant about excuses, so I think I'll skip it today," she said blithely, knowing that she'd taken a giant leap across the line, but not really giving a damn.

As her boss began another lecture about her obligations to the bank and being polite to her superiors, Jennifer heard the sound of Stetson's truck rumbling down from the barn and Greg's voice faded away completely.

She watched the truck come to a stop in front of the house.

Her heart skipped a beat.

At the very edge of her awareness, she could still hear Greg droning on and on. She refocused for a second to make sure her boss was still raving and not actually talking to her, but he sounded like he was just getting warmed up, so she went back to ignoring him.

Stetson slipped from the truck and, looking at her on the porch, he nodded once in acknowledgement before leaning back into the cab to gather something from the console. When his head reappeared, Jennifer's breathing quickened. The brooding storm clouds behind him threw his handsome figure into greater contrast, perfectly framed by the wilderness of the area. He belonged here. She had to make sure he stayed here.

"*Jennifer!*" Greg's voice leapt to the front of her attention.

"I'm sorry," Jennifer said, scrambling for a way to cover her inattention. "Ummm…you broke up there at the end. What was that last part?"

She watched as Stetson grabbed something from the bed of the truck, his hair plastered to his head from the rain. She wanted to run her fingers through it and straighten it out.

"I *saaaaiiiiiddddd*…the board wants options."

"I'm exploring that right now," Jennifer said, dropping her head in exasperation. "I have to see what assets—"

"Let me be frank," he cut in. "The board wants to know if foreclosure is an option."

"Well, yes, foreclosure is always an option," she replied at the same time she heard the sound of Stetson's boot hitting the porch step.

Her head snapped up. He was *not* smiling. There was no way Stetson missed hearing that last sentence.

Shit, shit, shit, shittiest shit of all shits.

She was screwed. She watched him storm past her into the house, the phone call completely forgotten in that instant.

Greg was still talking but for once, she didn't wait for him to stop.

"I got it, Greg," she said, talking over whatever the hell he was saying. "I'll get you and the board my recommendation as quickly as I can. I gotta go."

Jennifer hit the red button, ending the call. She turned and watched the screen door, still bouncing against the door frame from being slammed by Stetson.

She had *no* idea how to talk her way out of this one.

CHAPTER 20

STETSON

*H*E KNEW IT. He'd been thrown off there for a minute by her bright green eyes and how adorably tiny she was, like a Barbie doll come to life, but it'd all been an act. He'd known better, but he'd let his dick convince him otherwise.

Never listen to his dick. If he ever chose to get a tattoo, that should be what it read. Dad would've told him that he was being a dick by tattooing that to his body, but then again, Dad up and died on him, so Stetson wasn't real sure why he should care.

Abandoned, yet again, by someone who should've been there for him. His mom, his dad, Michelle, even his brothers…this farm was the only thing that was *his*, and here was this green-eyed asshole of a beauty, trying to take it away from him too.

Carmelita came out of the kitchen, drying her hands on a kitchen towel. "What is wrong?" she asked, peering up at his stormy face.

"I don't want to see her again," he growled, taking a perverse pleasure in being snarly and grumpy and rude to Carmelita. He shouldn't, but he liked it anyway. He was sick of being the good guy all the time. "If she ever comes back, she'd better do it when I'm not here. No food, no talking, nothing at all! She deserves nothing at all." It was satisfying to say that twice, to really mean it. To rub it in.

Jennifer Kendall really did deserve nothing at all. Nothing except the worst in life.

"She is the *enemy!*" he shouted. The phrase he'd been telling himself for three days now slipped out, unbidden, but that didn't make them any less true. She *was* the enemy. She pretended otherwise, but he knew better. He'd always known better, but with this last reminder...he wouldn't forget this time.

Never forget.

Carmelita's eyes widened but for once, he didn't wait to hear what she had to say. He stormed into the family room, past his father's recliner, and threw himself into his, turning on the TV and jacking up the sound until the walls were shaking.

Screw 'em all. Screw the whole world.

CHAPTER 21

JENNIFER

*O*KAY, *don't panic. I can go in and explain the situation to him. He has to listen to me. He has to realize that foreclosure is a real possibility at this point. It doesn't matter what I do or say, the possibility is out there and I may not be able to stop it.*

She took a step towards the front door and then stopped. He wasn't in the mood to listen to a word she said. She should give him space and deal with him in the morning. Maybe with some time to cool off, he'd be willing to hear her out.

She turned back to leave and then realized that except for her nylons, she was barefoot. No wonder she was so cold. Tiptoeing back, she eased the screen door and front door open as quietly as she could and retrieved her heels from just inside the house, where she'd kicked them off that morning.

Carmelita was saying something, her voice so quiet that the words were indistinguishable.

Shoes in hand, Jennifer backed away slowly.

Stetson said something in reply, and then... "She deserves nothing at all," Stetson yelled, his voice raw with hatred. "She is the *enemy!*"

Jennifer eased the doors shut, hastily slipped her shoes on, grabbed her bag from the rocking chair, and plunged into the rain. She practically threw herself into her car, mud and rain and tears mixing together into a soup of disaster and pain. Reaching into her bag, she rummaged around for her keys.

She had to get out of there. She had to go. She had to leave. Right now.

She found the keys. Fumbling, she finally got the right key in the ignition. Starting the car, she slammed the shifter into reverse and jammed her foot down.

Tears were already blurring her vision as she felt the wet gravel give way under the tires. Blindly, she slapped the shifter into drive and rocketed out of the farmyard.

"I am *not* the *enemy!*" she screamed, pounding the steering wheel.

The car slipped and then caught on the muddy road. Jennifer didn't notice. She thought back to how she'd reached up and stroked his cheek. She'd listened to him talk about his father fighting cancer, and she'd felt for him. She'd bandaged his hand.

Sure, "Foreclosure is always an option" wasn't the best statement in the world to overhear someone say, but didn't she deserve at least a *little* bit of grace? A chance to explain herself?

She flipped the windshield wipers on high, not sure if it was the moisture outside or the moisture in her eyes that was blurring the world. They flapped hard, swishing maniacally across the windshield, but still, she could see almost nothing.

Tears it was, then.

She wondered what Carmelita was thinking in that moment. Was she listening to Stetson describe what he'd overheard, and wondering why she'd ever been nice to such a traitor? The thought of Carmelita hating her…it hurt almost as much as Stetson's hatred.

"I am *not* the *enemy!*" she yelled again, pounding the steering wheel with every syllable.

She was already screaming when the front tire found a soft spot near the edge of the gravel road. The car jerked. The steering wheel twisted violently from her hands.

Terrified, Jennifer's body pulled into itself as the car and inertia took control. Her forehead slammed into the steering wheel, pain exploding outward from the impact. She screamed again.

The tire caught in the eroded drainage channel that paralleled the roadway, directing the car forward as it quickly slowed. Finally, with a sudden jerk, the car came to a stop pointing away from the road.

Panicked, her body still curled into a defensive position, she sat there, her heart hammering painfully against the inside of her ribcage.

She didn't know how much time had passed

before she dared to move. She gave herself a personal inventory. She extended her legs and wiggled her toes; she watched as she made fists with both hands and then stretched her fingers outward.

Finally, she reached up and readjusted the rearview mirror that had been knocked askew so that she could look at her face. She couldn't see any blood on her forehead, which she took as a good sign.

Luckily, she hadn't been driving that fast. Too fast for the conditions, sure, but not so fast that the crash caused serious damage. She probed the tender spot in the center of her forehead. *Ouch!* She should've been wearing her seatbelt. She was usually so good at putting it on, but today...today, she'd just been too pissed to think clearly.

Self-check complete, she looked around the car for her stuff. Spotting it, she leaned over and grabbed her computer bag from where it had fallen onto the passenger-side floor, and pulled it up onto her lap.

She dug around in the front pockets until she found her phone.

Thank God it isn't broken.

Then she realized that the phone was ringing. The screen read "Paul Limmer" before it turned itself off, the battery completely drained.

CHAPTER 22

STETSON

STETSON SHIFTED around, trying to find a comfortable place in his leather recliner. Usually super comfy, tonight he just couldn't find a good spot. Everything was lumpy and wrong and the wooden frame was digging into him.

Determined, Stetson shifted again, ignoring whatever was happening on the TV. Some sort of sports was on, although under threat of death, he couldn't begin to guess what it was, and didn't care. It was just serving as his signal to the world (i.e., Carmelita) to leave him the hell alone.

Finally, he found just the right spot and sank in, letting the tension go just a little bit. Perfect. He was now in a great position to fully enjoy a nice wallow in his funk…

Which was when he heard a knock on the front door.

Stetson didn't move. He wasn't in the mood to put on a cheerful face and anyway, Carmelita liked to greet people.

"It is your house, *Mr. Miller.* You can answer the door," Carmelita hollered from the kitchen.

Fine. Stetson sighed as he flipped up the handle releasing the foot rest, turning the volume down on the TV as he hoisted himself up. He'd never admit it to Carmelita, but the TV had honestly been hurting his ears. It had been just too damn loud, even for him.

When had he become such an old man?

Padding his way over to the front door in just his socks, he fully expected to find Declan or Wyatt, ready to tear into him now that they'd heard the news about the farm. To be perfectly honest, he was surprised they hadn't heard the news before now. Sawyer wasn't exactly the ideal town to try to hide news from others, good *or* bad. Just what he needed today – an ass-chewing from Wyatt.

Stetson's shoulders tightened up at the thought. If Wyatt said one word – *one word!* – about Stetson being the baby of the family, he wasn't sure he could be accountable for his actions after that. Wyatt deserved a can of whoop-ass to be delivered to him, anyway. Today was just the day to do it. In fact—

He jerked the heavy wooden door open, ready to tell Wyatt to just shut the hell up and get his nose out of places where it didn't belong, when instead, he found Jennifer.

A soaked Jennifer, hunched over and shivering from the cold.

Dammit, why is she here? Why isn't she in Franklin, eating dinner? Far, far away from me?

"What are you doing here?" he growled. He folded his arms over his chest and glared down at her. He leaned against the doorframe of the front door, blocking her entrance with his body. If she thought she would slip by him and into the house, she had another think a-comin'. She wasn't welcome, and he was *not* going to budge on that fact.

"The better question is, why are you still standing on the front porch, shivering like a newborn kitten in the middle of winter?" asked an angry Spanish-accented voice from behind him.

Double damn. He should've known that Carmelita wouldn't be able to resist coming to the door, even after ordering him to answer it. Nothing happened under *her* roof that she didn't know about.

"I told you how I felt about this situation earlier today," Stetson said over his shoulder to Carmelita through gritted teeth, "and that decision still stands."

Smack! Stetson's head lurched forward at the impact.

Every time Carmelita hit him on the back of the head, he had to wonder how a woman so short could reach so high.

"You have been rude enough for one day. I try to respect your feelings earlier today even if you were rude when you say them to me," Carmelita said furiously. "Now there is young woman on the porch who needs warm and shelter of your home. I do not care who she is or where she come from, *mi hijo*, you will be rude no more."

Carmelita's English, usually better than his, worsened the angrier she was. Based on the speech she just gave, she was *pissed*.

And *mi hijo*? That was just low. She rarely called him that, but when she did...

She played to win, he'd give her that.

"Come in and I will find you a towel," Stetson said in a voice so low, it was barely audible. He turned and slunk past Carmelita, his head still bent low.

"Come, come," he heard the elderly woman say.

Returning with the towel he'd found in the guest bathroom, Jennifer was telling her about spinning off the road as Carmelita was squeezing the water out of Jennifer's hair. Her jacket was hanging on a hook next to the door, dripping harmlessly onto the tile entryway. It was all for show and had obviously become soaked quickly, offering very little protection during her journey from wherever the hell she'd crashed her car.

Her white blouse was just as wet as the jacket, the thin white material clinging to her lace bra.

For just a second, Stetson forgot to be angry.

Blinking, trying to wipe the image from his mind, Stetson retrieved a raincoat from the alcove and handed it to her. Jennifer stared at him, resigned and disappointed.

He tugged on his boots and grabbed a second coat for himself from the row of hooks.

Carmelita was still fussing over her, grabbing the towel from Stetson's hand and rubbing Jennifer's hair with it.

"I will find you dry clothes. They will most likely not fit, but they will be dry. I will wash these and..."

"Before you get too dry, let's go," Stetson interrupted.

"Stetson Byron Miller!" Carmelita hollered.

"I need her to go back to the car with me," Stetson interrupted again before she could really get on a roll, "and steer while I pull it out of the ditch with the truck. I don't much see the point of getting her into dry clothes, just so she can get wet again."

"You'd do that for me?" Jennifer asked, astonished.

"Carmelita says that I've been rude to everybody today, and I probably have. Some of the people I have been rude to did not deserve it," he said, looking pointedly at Carmelita before turning back to Jennifer. "Some of those people probably did deserve it," he looked even more pointedly at Jennifer, "but I'm not going to leave you stuck on the side of the road in the rain overnight, no matter why the hell you're here."

Stetson looked at the drenched woman. She seemed so small in that moment. Trails of water traced down her cheeks. He desperately hoped that it was rainwater. Crying always made him very uncomfortable.

Very, *very* uncomfortable.

Dammit, I think those are tears…

CHAPTER 23

JENNIFER

THE DRIVE back to her car was uncomfortably quiet. That kind of quiet that makes a person want to break out into song, even if they're tone deaf, just so that *some* sort of noise was being made.

Couldn't the radio be playing something truly awful, like *She Thinks My Tractor's Sexy?* Or *The Watermelon Crawl?*

She knew she was desperate if she was willing to listen to *The Watermelon Crawl.*

But the radio was painfully silent and Stetson was painfully silent and the only noise was the swish of the wipers on the windshield and the growl of the engine and the spin of the tires as the rain-softened road slid and gave way beneath the giant tires of the truck.

Which had the unexpected side effect of making her feel slightly better, because if this truck was struggling, her little Civic had no chance at all, even if she *had* been driving with her mind totally on the task at hand.

Which she totally hadn't been, of course.

She mentally sorted through her choices, sparse as they were. For the past three days, she'd held her tongue. She'd thought that actions spoke louder than words, and she still believed that. But that long-held belief aside, she probably needed to face the facts: It was within the realm of possibility that a few words of explanation could go a long ways.

Orrrrr…they could do nothing at all.

But dammit all, she *had* to try. Then, at least, she wouldn't be playing the "What if?" game with herself for the next month.

Just as she was talking herself into talking, the rear end of her Honda appeared between the swipes of the wipers. *Wow.* She'd been so close to making it to the pavement. Another 50 yards, and she would've been long gone from the Miller farm.

Well, this was her sign – she had to talk now, before they got involved with the process of trying to pull the car out of the ditch. That would be chaotic and before she knew it, they'd have her car out of the ditch and Stetson would still not be talking to her and nothing would've changed. It was do-or-die time.

She opened up her mouth to speak.

"I'm going to have to pull you out backward," Stetson said flatly, cutting her off at the pass. Her mouth snapped shut. There was no emotion in his voice, as if he were reading a grocery list to a brick wall. "There's really no point of driving up to the road and turning around because you're going to have to do the same thing once we pull you out, so we might as well both do that once your car is back on the road."

"Okay," she said softly. *Don't chicken out, don't chicken out. Tell him what's going—*

"You stay here outta the rain while I get everything hooked up and then you can get in your car and steer while I pull."

"I need to tell you something!" she blurted out, before he could say anything else. Talking to Stetson Byron Miller was stupidly difficult to do, she was starting to realize.

"Yes?" Flat. Distant. He stared straight ahead, refusing to make eye contact.

"I know what you heard today sounded bad."

"Yeah, it sounded pretty damn bad." Taking his hand off the door handle, he turned towards her. His hard features were cast only in the light of the dashboard. She took a deep breath. She just had to get through this.

"I know you're not in the mood to believe me, but I need to tell you anyway: I don't want to take your farm away. My job is to come out here, look at your books, and see if there's a way for you to get caught up with the bank. That can range from selling equipment to selling a small piece of land to maybe even finding a different market for your crops that pays a higher amount. The possibilities are endless, and I'm here to help you work through those possibilities together. I'm *not* here to simply foreclose."

He was just staring at her. No emotion. Nothing at all. She wondered hysterically for a moment if she'd been inadvertently assigned to the first case of true artificial intelligence. Of course, a robot would've acted a lot more rationally over the past few days.

"Look, you can be 100% sure of that!" she exclaimed, inspiration striking. "If I was just going to recommend foreclosure, then why even audit your books, right? The bank could've just foreclosed and spared the expense of sending me out here. I get my hourly wage plus my hotel and a per diem every day that I'm out on an audit. It's expensive to do this. The bank doesn't have to send me, but they choose to, because they want to find a way for you to keep your farm."

"You'll have to excuse me if that sounds slightly insane," Stetson said sarcastically, the first emotion peeking through since they'd started this conversation. "Why not just take the farm? It'd make you a pretty penny on the auction block."

"Yes, that's true. *If* we can find a buyer who has deep enough pockets to buy an operation like this. Not everyone has millions of dollars laying around to buy a new farm. Hell, you wouldn't be able to buy this farm if you were starting out today. You only own it because you inherited it from your father."

"You do wonders for a man's pride, you know that?"

Jennifer chose to ignore that comment. "Also, you want to know where banks make their money? Interest. If they auction this farm off to the highest bidder, that bidder will be paying cash. They won't be borrowing from Intermountain. Which is a nice little pile of cash right now, but long-term, the bank makes a lot more money from a customer through interest."

"So why are you discussing foreclosure with some random guy on the phone?" he challenged her.

"That 'random guy' happens to be my boss. He... he doesn't always see the world the same way I do." She shrugged, her turn to stare out the front windshield, the methodical swishing of the wipers and pattering of the rain the only sound in the cab.

She could do this. She *would* do this.

"Look. Here's the truth: The bank only looks at the overall closure rate on our cases when deciding whether we were successful or not – in other words, whether my boss gets his Christmas bonus this year. That means the sooner we make it through a case and move onto the next, the more cases we can make it through in a year, and the better my boss looks. Even though the *bank* wants me to find a way for farmers and ranchers to be able to keep their property, my *boss*...not so much. He just wants me in, out, and on my way. A misalignment of incentives, honestly."

She paused for a moment to debate whether or not she should tell him everything – that even for her boss, he was being unreasonably pushy and demanding that she wrap things up quickly; that this particular case seemed strangely personal to Greg for reasons she couldn't even begin to fathom.

But before she could decide whether that was a good idea or would just feed into Stetson's paranoia about the bank being out to get him, he spoke.

"So, you're looking for a way for me to keep my farm?"

"Yes," she said with conviction.

"Okay," Stetson said, slapping the steering wheel lightly. "Let's get your car out of the mud."

Jennifer sat there, stunned, as she watched him hop out of the truck into the rain. Did he actually believe her? Or was he simply done listening to her "excuses"? Was he just trying to get through this so he could send her away?

What the hell does "okay" mean? Argh! I will never *understand men.*

CHAPTER 24

JENNIFER

*J*ENNIFER WAS LAUGHING as she burst through the front door of the farmhouse, shaking and stamping the water off onto the entryway tile. Carmelita came hurrying in to see what the commotion was all about, and stuttered to a halt when she spotted Jennifer.

"Did you get your car out of the mud?" she asked, her eyebrows wrinkling with concern as she took in Jenn's appearance.

Which even Jennifer had to admit was a bit on the dirty side. Still unable to control her giggles as she shucked the oversized raincoat off her shoulders, Jennifer looked at the housekeeper.

"Nope, it's still stuck," she said cheerfully.

"Where is Stetson?"

"He went 'round the back of the house. He said you'd be mad if he came through the front door."

Jennifer barely got the words out before another round of laughter overtook her.

Carmelita was completely confused.

"What is so funny about going out in the rain? And why would I care what door he comes in?"

"Because of the mess," Stetson said, emerging from the back of the house.

Carmelita turned and Jennifer's laughter stopped abruptly. Stetson was wearing just a pair of jeans, slung low on his hips. Jennifer's mouth instantly went dry.

"Why are you half naked?" Carmelita demanded. "Nobody wants to see you like that."

Speak for yourself, lady.

He was even better looking without a shirt on than Jennifer would've guessed. He wasn't a gym rat, with weirdly bulging muscles all over his body, but rather, long, sleek muscles that danced over his body like trails of pleasure that Jennifer would love to follow.

But shouldn't. Totally, absolutely shouldn't.

Her eyes snapped to the floor instead and she kept her gaze glued there as Stetson protested, "I figured you'd want a half-naked Stetson over a muddy one. These were the only clothes I could find in the laundry room."

Carmelita harrumphed, and Jennifer bit back her laughter. She'd only been at the Miller Farm for three days, and she already knew that this was Carmelita's way of admitting he was right, without actually saying it out loud. She might be sweet and loving, but she also had as much pride as her adopted son.

They were quite the pair, really.

"How did you become so dirty?" Carmelita asked, clearly wanting to change the topic back to the one she cared about. "You even have mud in your hair!"

Jennifer couldn't help it – she had to look up again. Sure enough, there were streaks of mud on him where his careless swipes with a towel had missed, along with one large chunk on his chiseled cheekbone. Jennifer's giggles returned at the housekeeper's outraged tone of voice.

"He fell," Jennifer managed to choke out through her laughter.

"Yeah, I fell and slid down the side of the road into the borrow pit," he admitted with a wry grin. "My jeans, coat, and even my shirt are covered in mud. You should see the inside of my truck!" Which was when the craziness of the situation hit him as well, and he began to laugh, deep and rusty, as if he'd long ago forgotten how to.

At first, Jennifer had been horrified as she'd watched from the safety and oh-so-wonderful dryness of the truck cab as his feet had lost traction, and he'd slid down the side of the road on his ass, landing with a splash in the water running down the ditch.

But when he'd struggled to his feet and began trying to make his way back up the short incline, she'd begun to laugh. He'd been reduced to crawling on all fours up the rain-softened ditch bank that kept giving way under his weight. By the time he'd gotten back up on the road, he was completely covered in mud from head to toe, back and front. He'd looked like some bizarre mud monster from an eight-year-old boy's dream.

"I am happy you did not cover my clean floor in mud," Carmelita sniffed. "Now, go put some clothes on while I find something for Jennifer to wear while I wash her clothes." Before she left, she turned back and caught Jennifer's eye. She was smiling, her face glowing with warmth and happiness.

It suddenly struck Jenn that there had been little reason to laugh in the Miller household for a very long time. She wondered when it was that Carmelita had last seen Stetson laugh.

Probably years.

As the housekeeper's footsteps faded away, Jennifer began twisting her hair, squeezing out a small stream of water onto the tile floor. She shouldn't have jumped out of the cab – standing on the side of the road and watching Stetson climb the ditch bank hadn't exactly helped him get up to the top any faster, and had only meant that in the end, she was as soaked as he was – but it'd been instinctual. Watching him struggle from the cab of the truck would've been cheating.

And really, after her hike through the rain back to the Miller farmhouse in the first place, she'd gotten plenty soaked on her own. Her second bath just sealed the deal.

Lifting her head, she froze. Stetson had crossed the room to stand in front of her – he was entirely too quiet for her sanity – and she realized with a stab of panic that they were alone. Her, him, and his very delicious chest. She had a hard time tearing her eyes away from his abs. She wanted to run her fingers up his chest and…

Her face grew red and she snapped her eyes up to his. She had to keep eye contact with him.

Don't look down, don't look down, don't look down…

"We'll get your car out tomorrow," Stetson said in his low, gravelly voice that sent shivers down her spine. Or maybe it was the cold clothes and wet hair. It was hard to tell at this point. "I might have to use a tractor," he continued, oblivious to her internal distress. Unlike her, he didn't seem to be the least bit affected by their proximity. Or his half-naked state of being. "I don't know what Carmelita is making for dinner, but I'm sure there'll be enough for an army. You okay with staying here tonight?"

She couldn't speak. Words were a thing, and they should totally be used, but she couldn't remember how.

Her eyes locked on to his lips. They looked soft. She focused on the small wrinkles and the line of his upper lip that rose and fell. His mouth reminded her of the outline of the distant mountain range outside.

The chunk of mud on his cheek was driving her crazy. She wanted to reach up and pluck it off but she didn't dare cross that line. Well, cross it again.

And spend the night under the same roof as this gorgeous man? Her tongue darted out to wet her lips. She was pretty sure it was going to be a sleepless night of staring at the ceiling for her.

Finally, she managed to nod her head. She was quite proud of herself for being able to do that, really.

"Good. I'm gonna go take a shower – I'm sure I missed some mud somewhere. Carmelita won't let me near the table like this," he said and walked away, the W's on the back pockets of his jeans bouncing up and down hypnotically as he went.

She could be the one to wash the mud from his hair and cheek. She could run her fingers through his hair and across his chiseled cheekbone...

I wonder how literal he was being when he said the jeans were the only *clothing in the laundry room.*

She felt her face warm in spite of the cold rainwater that still covered her.

CHAPTER 25

STETSON

STETSON PULLED BACK the chair for Jennifer, and then sat down kitty-corner from her, the light from the elk horn chandelier overhead dancing in her dark locks. A platter of steaming steak strips, a plate of homemade tortillas, and all of the fixin's were spread out in front of them. A batch of homemade salsa, just made yesterday, was sitting proudly between them. Carmelita had been sure to inform them of its freshness, before disappearing.

"Is she coming back?" Jennifer asked as he began to dish up the taco ingredients. She was looking around, as if expecting Carmelita to jump out from behind the china hutch or something. Stetson's mouth quirked up at the corners at the idea.

"She usually eats dinner with me, but tonight, she said she had some errands to run." Stetson was pretty damn sure the "errand" she had to run was, "Hide from Jennifer and Stetson so they could fall in love," but he was *not* about to tell Jennifer that. Carmelita had never pulled this disappearing act when he'd brought Michelle home, that was for damn sure. There had been a few times when Carmelita had practically guarded the homestead, trying to run Michelle off before she even dared to come down the gravel driveway.

Stetson only hoped that Carma had packed up some of this spread to take back to her cottage, so she didn't have to cook dinner twice tonight. That didn't seem awfully fair, especially after how he'd treated her the last couple of days. He winced at the recollection.

"Are you okay?" Jennifer's soft voice broke into his thoughts, and he jerked, sending her a smile before he even really registered her words.

"Oh yeah, just…thinking about what a long day this has been." Which was about as close to the truth as he was willing to admit. Before Jennifer could bring everything up all over again and really rub in how wrong he'd been, he hurried on. "I've been meaning to ask you – you said that you quit the nursing profession because of Paul? Or was it Greg?"

"Paul. Greg is my boss at the bank."

"Right. Because *Paul* cheated on you with other nurses."

She bobbed her head as she took a bite of the taco, her eyes drifting shut as she made a sound of pure pleasure. The sound sent a bolt of lust straight to Stetson's dick, and he shifted in his chair, trying to remember how to breathe. And talk. They were talking. About something.

Her tongue darted out, snagging an errant piece of cilantro off her lip, and Stetson almost let out a groan of his own. She was going to be the death of him.

"Well, you…he…it's just…"

Finally, her eyes opened and she looked over at him, her brow creased with confusion. "Yes?" she asked. She probably thought he was having a stroke.

A stroke caused by lust. Was that a thing? It totally seemed like it was a thing.

He shifted again in his suddenly uncomfortable chair. "Why switch professions?" he got out in a rush. He cleared his throat and continued on. "I understand not wanting to work with Paul anymore. But why not just go work for a different doctor's office? Or hospital? Why become an accountant? It seems pretty drastic." Of course, Stetson was born a farmer, raised a farmer, and someday, would die a farmer. The idea of letting someone else dictate which profession he worked in seemed…bizarre to him.

"Hmmm…" She licked her fingers on her right hand, cleaning off the juice from the tasty tacos. She was *not* helping with his sanity levels, that was for damn sure.

"You know, it's funny because in retrospect, that's such a good point. Honestly, I was pretty young, and was only a peon in the medical world. I was pulling 18-hour days and overnight shifts and wasn't getting paid much, in comparison to the workload, but I'd had this idea that I just had to push through, Paul would become a doctor, and then I could afford to go to school to become an RN. That would have meant a significant pay increase for me. Instead, I'd worked my fingers to the bone, all to support a guy who actually thought I'd buy the excuse that he was teaching Lizzie 'mouth to mouth resuscitation' when I found them in bed together. Do I *look* that stupid to you?" She let out a snort of laughter that had Stetson grinning, despite the seriousness of the topic. He had a sudden urge to rearrange the guy's face, and he hadn't even met him.

For Paul's sake, he had to hope he never would.

"Anyway, looking back on it…nursing was never my passion. I thought I'd grow to love it over time because I enjoy helping people, but blood and guts and poop? Not exactly the stuff dreams are made of."

"Poop?" he repeated in disbelief.

"People shit themselves all the time," Jennifer said with a shrug.

Stetson choked as he looked down at the remains of his taco on his plate. Brown and red, with bits of green…

"Probably not appropriate dinner conversation," she said with a weak smile, which had Stetson busting up.

So much laughter. Did everyone laugh this much? Or did this only happen around Jennifer Kendall?

Was she some sort of laughter fairy, sprinkling joy everywhere she went?

She can't be trusted. She's here to steal your farm away from you.

But for the first time, he absolutely knew that wasn't true. Sitting here across the table from her, listening to her talk about shit and Paul and blood, there was something completely trustworthy about her. It rather terrified him, actually – to believe someone wholeheartedly, especially someone he'd thought only days before was nothing short of the devil incarnate. Logically, he knew he shouldn't trust her. Shouldn't believe her. Should hold her at arm's length.

There were a lot of shoulda, coulda, woulda's in the world, but this time, Stetson was willing to trust his gut.

At least for now.

CHAPTER 26

JENNIFER

*J*ENNIFER STOLE a sideways glance at the stupidly handsome farmer to her left, wondering why she'd just told him all of that. He probably thought she deserved to get her heart broken by Paul. After all, she was the enemy, right?

But as his dimples flashed in the elk horn chandelier lighting – *who decorates with elk horns?!* – she realized that he truly did seem to have started to believe her. He wasn't holding back. He wasn't waiting for her to let her guard down so he could tear her to shreds.

He actually believed her.

She was in shock, to be honest. She wasn't used to men believing her. That had started with Paul, of course, but Greg didn't help matters, either. Believing her because she said so?

It was a heady feeling.

They stood up to begin clearing off the table, and Jennifer cast about for something to say. "I've been meaning to ask – why did you inherit the Miller Farm? I don't know much about farms, but even I know that the oldest son usually inherits. Did your brothers just not want to farm? Do they do something else?"

Stetson scraped the bits and pieces off the plates and into the trash, then stacked the dishes neatly in the sink. Carmelita had him well trained.

"Nope, they both own farms of their own, actually. My dad helped with the financing for both of them, putting his name on their deeds and co-signing on their loans so Goldfork Credit Union would take them seriously."

"They borrowed money from a different bank?!" Jennifer said with a pretended huff of indignation. Stetson opened up his mouth to apologize or defend the decision or something, but she shot him a huge grin. "I'm just kidding. I always wondered why you guys borrowed from Intermountain, considering the nearest branch is in Boise."

Stetson snagged a beer out of the fridge – a dark, bitter-looking thing – and held one up for her. She shook her head. "Wine?" he asked, sticking his head back in the fridge. "I have a riesling in here somewhere."

"Sure!" she said. "A glass of riesling would be nice." She shouldn't be drinking wine with a client, but she also shouldn't be eating dinner with them or flirting with them or spending the night at their house, so she figured one more "shouldn't" wouldn't hurt her at this point.

He popped the cork on the bottle and filled a glass for her – a huge goblet, actually – and she took it hesitantly. If she drank all of this, she'd be slobbering drunk by the end of it.

She'd have to take it slow. Small sips. At least she wasn't driving tonight, right?

"My grandfather had a dispute with Goldfork Credit Union back in the day," Stetson said, jerking Jennifer back to their conversation she'd mostly forgotten they'd been having. Picking up his beer with his bandaged hand, he led the way to the living room. "He vowed to never bank there again. I do believe that the offending charge was a quarter." He shot her a self-deprecating grin. "I like to think that I came by my stubbornness naturally."

She let out a loud chuckle as they settled into a plush, welcoming couch. A brick fireplace with a thick wooden beam serving as the mantle was in front of them, but because it was July, Carmelita had put a decorative candle holder in the hearth instead of stacking up logs. Stetson caught her studying the intricate metalwork of the candle holder, and pushed himself off the couch. "I always mean to do this but never actually do. It's nicer to look at than a TV any ol' day of the week." He pulled a lighter out of a vase on the mantle and set about lighting the candles. The flickering glow instantly added a warmth to the room...or maybe it was the wine. She always had been a lightweight.

For some reason, she took another sip of the wine, because in that moment, it *totally* seemed like a good idea.

"By the time my brothers were ready to borrow for their farms," Stetson continued, settling back down on the couch next to her, "my grandfather had passed away and my brothers wanted to do business locally, instead of driving back and forth to Boise for every little thing. I just stuck with Intermountain because...well, I don't know. Old habits die hard, I suppose."

"So your brothers bought their own farms, and you inherited this one?"

Stetson rearranged the pillows behind him for a moment, fussing with their placement, his internal debate stamped clearly on his face. She wondered how much he'd eventually choose to tell her, and how much he'd hold back. "I can't pretend my brothers were happy about this," he said finally, staring into the flickering white globe candles. "They weren't. It caused a lot of problems, actually. Wyatt – he's the oldest – and I...we never got along. But after I inherited the farm, lock, stock, and barrel, things didn't exactly become better between us." He took a long sip of his beer. "If he knew you were here...if he knew what was going on with the bank payment..." He let out a bitter laugh. "You think *I* have a bad temper? You should meet Wyatt. He makes a jumping cactus look as welcoming as a cold beer on a hot day in comparison."

"If you ever want to see the true strength of a family, just start discussing who inherits what after a death," Jennifer said with a small grin. "Banking is pretty boring for the most part, but I once saw a fistfight break out between an uncle and niece over who got to keep the fully restored two-door 1966 Chevy Nova."

"Niece?" Stetson repeated with a startled laugh.

"Yup. And she had a pretty good right hook, actually. Laid her uncle out in the foyer of the bank. I was just glad that I was calling the police to report a fight, not a bank robbery."

"I think you're taking that 'Be grateful for everything' mantra a little too far," Stetson said dryly.

Jennifer shrugged. "It's not hard to be an optimist when life generally goes my way."

"You mean, when your boyfriend uses you for years to pay for his schooling, and then cheats on you once he's actually made it as a doctor? That kind of good luck?"

"I didn't say *everything* in my life goes my way," she protested, her cheeks warming with embarrassment. He made her sound so Pollyanna. She wasn't; she just chose to look on the bright side of life.

"What about that time you got assigned to audit a jackass of a farmer who made your life miserable, and then you got your car stuck in a muddy ditch while trying to leave his sorry ass behind?"

"Hmmm…I think you're right," Jennifer said, pretending to be serious for a moment. "I mean, have you met that guy? A real turd in the punchbowl."

"Turd in the punchbowl!" Stetson howled, clutching at his chest in pain. "I'm sure he's *nothing* like that!"

"Hey, I was just agreeing with you." She shot him a triumphant grin. "Are you trying to say that your summation of his character wasn't accurate?"

He paused, his beer bottle halfway up to his mouth. "I'm not quite sure how I got myself into this," he grumbled as he took another long swig.

"I couldn't begin to guess!" she informed him cheerily, holding her glass up to toast him. "I was just being a well-behaved guest, agreeing with my host." She batted her eyelashes innocently as she took another sip of her own drink.

It was heady and strong and she felt another flush of heat wash over her body. She wondered for a moment if she should stop and go to bed and hide from this man who set her on fire with just a look, but he was taking her glass out of her hand instead, and she just watched it go, a little off-balance from the missing weight of the goblet.

And then he was kissing her.

Finally kissing her.

It felt like years that she'd been waiting for this moment – decades, maybe – the electricity crackling between them like lightning strikes on a beach. It was hot and painful and amazing and she wasn't sure if she'd ever breathe right again. His mouth moved over hers, his tongue probing the seam of her lips, and then she was opening her mouth with a groan that mingled with his, as his tongue swept inside, wild and passionate. Her hands clutched at his shirt, trying and failing to hold onto something that would stabilize her. Ground her.

He was hovering over her and she realized that at some point, he'd laid her back on the couch and she hadn't even realized it had happened but instead of pushing him away as she should, instead of slapping him or kneeing him in the balls or *something*, she pulled harder on his shirt, tugging him towards her, wanting his weight on her, pressing her down, telling her that he wanted her too.

There was something that she should be worried about; some reason why having him take off her shirt wasn't a good idea, but it was fuzzy and out of reach and so Jennifer ignored it. She only wanted to focus on this man and this moment. Nothing else mattered.

For one glorious heartbeat, his hard body was pressed along the length of hers and he was working the buttons of her shirt, trying to open it up to his mouth and hands and gaze, and then he was gone.

Gone.

Where had he gone?

Jenn's eyes shot open – she hadn't even realized she'd closed them – and she sat up, chest heaving, collapsing against the back of the couch as Stetson stared at her, wide-eyed.

"I shouldn't have…I have to…goodnight."

He scrambled off the couch like his ass was on fire, and had made it to the doorway of the living room before turning back to say, "Up the stairs. First door on the left. That's your room."

And then he was gone and she was left alone, just her and the flickering candles in the hearth and a mostly empty glass of wine.

CHAPTER 27

STETSON

*H*E HEARD her stirring around long before she came down the stairs. He was sitting at the kitchen table, breakfast finished, doing his best to pretend as if everything was fine and normal, while Carmelita puttered around, humming happily to herself. Never one to miss a thing, she'd asked if he wanted fresh candles placed in the hearth for tonight, and he'd told her thank you, but no. She'd looked at him for a long moment, probably trying to decide how far she could press the questioning, but finally left it alone, going back to making breakfast for her and Jennifer.

Stetson could only hope that Jennifer liked to eat first thing in the morning, because Carma was cooking even more than normal, and that was truly saying something.

Finally, Jennifer stumbled down the stairs in a pair

of basketball shorts and a t-shirt, both relics leftover from Stetson's junior high years, and instantly, Stetson found that he had two competing thoughts in his head:

1) Why had Carmelita kept that clothing all this time? She surely didn't expect to need to clothe an accountant years down the road who didn't have the good grace to grow to a normal adult-sized height, and Stetson was surely never going to fit into those clothes again; and
2) Jennifer made basketball shorts and beat-up t-shirts look good. Damn good. Way too damn good.

He took a long sip of his coffee as he shifted in his chair, trying to hide his sudden arousal.

Yeah right. Who was he kidding? His arousal had never really left. After he'd run up the stairs last night and away from the temptation that was Jennifer the Accountant, he'd tried to take care of business the same way he always did, but the spark was missing after all these years, and the palm of his hand just wasn't the date it used to be, dammit, especially all wrapped up in the ace bandage Carmelita was faithfully replacing every morning.

The cuts were clean and infection-free, sure, but the bandage did tend to put a damper on…certain activities.

"Good morning," Jennifer said in a gravelly voice, jerking Stetson back to the present. She cleared her throat as she shoved her hair out of her face. "How are you guys this morning?" She had this crease across her face where her pillow must've been pressing into her cheek, and her hair was definitely on the mussed side.

Stetson shifted again. He wanted to be the cause of her looking like that. He wanted to see her with her lips wrapped around—

"Good, good," Carmelita said, breaking into Stetson's increasingly naughty thoughts. "Here, have some coffee, and I have an omelet almost done."

Jennifer slid into the other chair at the worn kitchen table, the one where Carmelita always sat, and the sight made Stetson feel distinctly...something. Uncomfortable? Happy? At peace? Disturbed? Horny?

Definitely something.

The accountant should not be sitting in Carmelita's chair in his old athletic clothes – without a bra, he was pretty sure – with mussed hair and a sleep line criss-crossing her face.

Absolutely, positively should not be happening.

Which was probably why he was having a hard time breathing. That had to be it.

"So what are you going to do today?" she asked him, clearly fishing around for a safe topic. "Has it stopped raining yet?" She craned her neck to look out the window over the kitchen sink, but he doubted that she could see much from her viewpoint.

"Cleared out a couple of hours ago," he

answered, glad to have a non-bra-and-mussed-hair topic to concentrate on. "Hopefully no more rain this summer, especially not like that."

Carmelita slid a plate overflowing with food in front of Jennifer, whose eyes were the size of saucers at the sheer amount of food in front of her. Stetson bit back a grin. Apparently, Jennifer didn't eat enough food for three grown men every morning. Considering how tiny she was, he couldn't say that he was overly surprised by that. Carma probably thought she needed to be fattened up. She was just perfect, by way of Stetson's thinking. He could pick her up and slide her down—

"I thought farmers liked rain," Jennifer said, confusion wrinkling her brow.

Stetson blinked for a moment, trying to remember what they were talking about.

"Right. They do. But not that much, all at once. Rain should water your crops, not drown them."

"Fair enough," Jennifer said, flashing a grin at him as she dug lustily into the plate in front of her. Carmelita clucked her approval as she watched Jenn go to town on her breakfast.

"Wyatt and Declan are coming over this afternoon to talk about harvest," Stetson continued. "Wyatt was supposed to be harvesting right away because of the drought we were in – his dryland wheat was ripening faster than normal because of that – but now...I don't know how he'll want to deal with it, now that his wheat is drenched. Dryland farming is a bitch sometimes." He shrugged, just as Carmelita snapped him across the head with the kitchen towel. "Dryland farming is downright *awful* sometimes!" he amended quickly. Carma gave him a pleased smile as Jennifer bit back a smile of her own.

Women…some days…

"Why does a drought cause wheat to ripen faster?" Jennifer asked, doggedly working her way through her plate of food. Stetson was quite impressed with her tenacity, actually.

"Evolution," Stetson said with a shrug and another sip of his coffee. He'd long ago finished his breakfast and should be getting work done, but chatting with Jenn was more fun.

Probably too much fun, but he was going to ignore that fact for the moment.

"If wheat isn't getting enough water," he continued, "it will put all of its energy towards producing the kernels, because that's its seed. Genetically, it wants to produce as much seed as possible before it dies, so a plant going through a drought will almost always stop any unnecessary growth, like leaves or roots, and focus only on developing their seeds as much as possible. How is it that you know so much about how much beef should cost, but not about how drought affects plants?"

She stopped with her fork halfway to her mouth, surprised by his brisk change in topic. "Oh. Well, because of my job. I go to farms and ranches and audit their books, to see if I can find anything of value to sell. I also make sure that all past deals are legit. Sometimes, people like to cook the books by over- or under-representing a sale, to either make themselves look more or less attractive to a bank, depending on their end goal."

Stetson cocked an eyebrow at her, confused. She sighed.

"So, let's say a rancher says that they're selling beef on the hoof for two dollars less than the going rate. Either he's a really bad businessman – which is possible – or he's lying and trying to hide income from the bank. If I don't know the going rate for beef on the hoof, then I'd look at that figure and not realize that it was potentially a lie. So when I got hired at Intermountain, I quickly started paying attention to the markets. But the amount of water on crops affecting when it needs to be harvested doesn't really enter the equation, so I haven't had to learn about it." She shrugged.

"Huh. Makes sense." He scratched at his stubble-covered jaw. It was such a different way of looking at things, and yet it made perfect sense how she could be totally ignorant and totally intelligent about the same topic at the same time. It hurt his head a little, truthfully. "You wanna see a cattle operation in action?"

He had no idea where that question came from. Certainly not from him. It was his voice, and it was his mouth moving, sure. But *he* wouldn't make that offer to Jennifer. Despite the fact that he trusted that she wanted to help him save his farm, that didn't mean that she would actually be able to. There was no guarantee. So dating someone in that position – who held that kind of power over him – was an insanely bad idea.

Which was why he'd run last night. A small part of his brain still seemed to be keeping up with reality, which was that Jennifer and Intermountain West Bank & Loan held his future in their hands, and they may just choose to squash him flat.

Unfortunately, the part of his brain that was keeping up with that reality seemed to be growing smaller by the day.

"Oh!" Jennifer stared at him over her coffee cup. Carmelita had disappeared somewhere, leaving just the two of them in the kitchen, and as the electricity crackled between them, the fact that they were alone seemed to be all he could think about.

Well, that and some other things, of course.

Jennifer swallowed hard, licking her lips. Stetson held his breath. The clock ticked on the wall.

"Yeah! I mean, sure. Yes. That'd be good." She took another sip of her coffee.

"Great!" he said, a little too cheerfully. He groaned inwardly. He sounded like a randy teenage boy who'd just convinced a girl to go on a date with him.

Which was probably a little closer to the truth

than his pride wanted to admit, although he wasn't sure how much of a date a city girl would consider the tour of a working farm to be.

"Let me go get your car out of the ditch first," he said quickly, trying to cover his nerves, "and then I can take you on a tour of the farm. Hold on – did you bring any clothes with you that *aren't* skirts or pantyhose or something?"

"I didn't bring any clothes with me at all. That's why I'm wearing your basket—"

"Not to the farm, here to Sawyer," he clarified. "Did you just bring auditing clothes to Sawyer?"

"Oh. Right. Ummm…yes. I don't normally pack any play clothes while I'm on an audit."

He had to work hard to keep from rolling his eyes. Jeans and boots were *not* play clothes. They were work clothes. The skirts and high heels – now those were the impractical ones. Although he would admit that it seemed like a stretch to call them play clothes, either. They were good for looks only, by his estimation.

She did look good in them, but that was besides the point.

"Hold on – how much longer are you going to be here?" he asked bluntly. He couldn't believe he hadn't thought to ask that question before. When she'd first arrived, he'd been blindly hoping she'd be gone by the end of the day, but it was Friday now, and she was still here. Didn't she need to go back to Boise at some point?

"An audit can last anywhere from one to two

weeks, depending on what I find," she said, shrugging. Stetson gulped. He was glad she hadn't informed him of that fact when she'd first arrived. He really would've blown a gasket.

Now, the idea of her sticking around for another week was terrifyingly thrilling, like being poised at the top of a steep drop on a rollercoaster ride at Six Flags.

Or what he assumed a rollercoaster ride would feel like. His parents hadn't exactly taken him to amusement parks every weekend growing up.

"The more complicated the business, the longer it takes. Or the messier an office, the longer it takes." She sent him a teasing grin. He grimaced in return.

"My filing skills aren't…exactly top notch." Which was his way of acknowledging that they plain didn't exist, and apologizing for that fact, guy style.

She shrugged. "Most farmers aren't. I would've been surprised if your office had been spick and span."

My office. That seemed so weird to hear. It was his office, even if it still didn't feel like it.

Would never feel like it.

"Well, I'll get to work on your car, if you want to get to work on the audit. I'll come get you when the Honda is out of the ditch."

Her eyebrows creased with concern. "Are you sure? You don't need me to drive it or something? I hate to have caused you a mess that you have to clean up."

"Nah, it's all good. I'll have Christian help me. He

was already done for the day when you showed up on the front porch last night, or I would've had him help me then. I try not to call him out after-hours."

"Who's Christian?" she asked, confused.

"My foreman. Him and a couple of other guys live full-time here on the farm; my other employees are seasonal. Christian's father, Jorge, is my brother's foreman, but I stole Christian away a long time ago with the siren call of handmade tamales." He'd seen Carmelita coming in through the doorway behind Jennifer, and had known that she'd love the compliment.

He was right. Of course.

"Christian is a good boy. He knows good food when he tastes it," Carmelita said with a wink, swooping in to grab their dishes and begin cleaning up. "Wyatt does not have a housekeeper, so he cannot bribe people to work for him with tasty food."

"He sure ain't gonna cook it himself," Stetson mumbled. The idea of his brother putting on an apron and cooking a meal was ridiculous. Wyatt was more likely to actually smile than he was to put on a frilly apron.

And God knows, Wyatt wasn't real likely to actually smile.

"Well, I better get to it," Jennifer said. "If I'm going to tour the farm, I should get more paperwork sorted before then. And hey, maybe with a tour of the farm, I might be able to spot something that could help with the bank loan."

As she headed upstairs to the guest room to get ready for the day, all Stetson could think was that if she told him to sell his truck, all bets were off. He was willing to do a lot of things for his farm, but that wasn't one of them.

CHAPTER 28

JENNIFER

*J*ENNIFER STARED down at the pile of clothes on the edge of the bed – they were her clothes from yesterday, clean and dry and pressed, courtesy of Carmelita. She'd never had a live-in housekeeper before, or even a maid who came and cleaned once a week, but Jenn was quickly starting to realize the benefits of such an arrangement.

Of course, if she continued to eat omelets and bacon strips and English muffins and diced fruit and handmade jelly every morning, she was going to need help walking pretty soon. Maybe they could just roll her from place to place. It would totally be worth it.

She pulled her skirt and white button-up shirt back on, and looked down with a sigh. It was true that this had to be the least practical outfit possible to tour a farm in. It may be clean right now, but she was pretty sure that thirty minutes in, it will have lost that crisp, clean look. Not to mention tramping through the mud in her high heels.

Farm tours were not normally part and parcel of an audit, but then again, neither was drinking wine or staying at a client's house or making out with said client on the couch or…

She forced those thoughts away. It'd been hard enough to fall asleep last night. Reliving those glorious moments on the couch was *not* going to help her concentrate on her job.

She looked around the beautiful guest room with a happy sigh. The roses on the wall, the fireplace, the hardwood floors – it was like a decorator's idea of what an old-fashioned farmhouse should look like, but with the patina of age and use that no decorator could ever fully imitate.

She had just stepped into the guest bathroom when she noticed that Carmelita had put a fresh toothbrush and toothpaste in there for her, for which Jennifer was wildly grateful. She could live through a lot of things, but unbrushed teeth was *not* one of them.

As her eyes traveled around the bathroom, she noticed a matching sliding door that she hadn't seen last night, directly across from the door she'd just come through. Curious, she slid it open to find a much more masculine guest bedroom, ready and made up to be used at a moment's notice. No painted roses this time, but rather, it was done up in dark blues accented with some lighter blues and cherry wood. It seemed to scream masculinity to Jennifer as she looked around. *Was this Stetson's room growing up?*

With a flush of embarrassment, she backed up into the bathroom, sliding the door shut again. She shouldn't be poking around in a client's home, no matter how much he had stopped feeling like a client, and had started feeling like a friend. Or more than a friend, actually.

She walked over to the vanity and set about brushing her teeth and getting ready for the day. Now was *not* the time to have those thoughts. She had a farm to save, dammit.

CHAPTER 29

STETSON

*H*E APPROACHED the door to his dad's office quietly, not wanting to disturb Jenn from her work, even though necessity dictated that he would; it didn't mean he had to want to. She was *not* going to be happy when she heard his news.

He peeked in to find her bent over the desk, her back to the door, mumbling as she ran the adding machine, the tape spitting out the top and curling every which way over the scarred desktop. The clanking noises from the calculator reminded him so much of his dad. He blinked, and there was his father, his reading glasses on the end of his nose, mumbling to himself as he fed numbers into the adding machine, his shoulders stooped with age and pain.

A stab of heartache tore through Stetson and he gasped at the pain. He missed his father so damn much sometimes…

The gasp must've been louder than he realized,

because Jennifer jerked her head around and spotted him in the doorway. She managed to extricate herself from the Fainting Goat Chair without falling down on the floor, and sent him a big smile. "Did you get my car out?" she asked, leaning against the desk with a coffee mug in hand. He watched the way her skirt tightened against her thighs, and gulped.

"Uhhhh…" he mumbled, tearing his eyes away from her thighs. *Bad news. I have bad news to deliver.* "So, I have bad news to deliver." *Way to ease into it, jackass.* He sent her an overly bright smile. Her eyes were widening with panic, and he rushed on. "I broke your car!" he blurted out.

Which, in retrospect, probably wasn't the easing into the topic that he could have done. She gasped and stared at him, thumping the coffee cup onto the desk next to her, brown liquid slopping out onto the desk. "You *what*?!" she practically hollered.

He sent her a painful smile. "Yeah. Broken. Ummm…not all of the parts are still attached to your car."

"What parts are not still attached?!" Her voice broke, squeaking like a pre-teen boy at the end of that question. He winced.

"Well, the mud had hardened once the rain stopped, and it turns out, the car was in there pretty deep. I was so close to getting it out, so I gave it one last yank, and…only the bumper came out."

"So my car is still in the ditch?" She was just

staring at him like he'd killed her kitten. He gulped again.

"No, no, the car is out. Christian got the backhoe and pushed on the backend while I tugged on the front end. He's loading it up onto a flatbed right now – he's going to drive it over to Mike's place to be fixed."

"Hold on, who's Mike?"

"Oh. Right." *She doesn't have every person in town memorized, jackass.* Which made him a jackass for a second time in the same conversation. He was on a roll. "Mike the Mechanic," he clarified. "He owns the best mechanic shop in town. His daughter does all of his paperwork for him. Good guy. His wife died years ago from cancer but he still owns the shop and is hard at work every day."

Annnnddddd...I'm going to shut up now. When even he could tell he was rambling, that wasn't a good sign.

"You broke my car," Jennifer repeated in disbelief. "I can't believe…" She broke out into laughter.

Laughter. Why was she laughing? It was his turn to just stare at her.

"This is a whole new level of insanity, you know that?" she got out. "I've never had a client break my car before. Just think – this audit is breaking all sorts of records. I've never spent the night at a client's house, I've never kissed a client—" his ears went bright red, but she just kept going, ticking the items off on her fingers as she went, "—I've never gotten my car stuck in the ditch, and I've never had a client break my car. So! An audit for the record books."

She sent him a brilliant, laughing smile, and he finally groped his way to the realization that she wasn't pissed. She wasn't ready to punch him or call him a bastard or knee him in the nuts. She was...

She was *fine*.

"Aren't you angry?" he burst out. He thought she'd made his head hurt before; that was nothing compared to what she was doing to it right now.

"Well, I can't say that it was the happiest, most awesome news I've ever heard in my life," she said with a shrug of her shoulders, "but eh, it's just a car. Mike the Mechanic – great name, by the way – will put it back together again. It'll go down the road again. Life will go on. I mean, I like my Honda, but it's just a thing – an item that can be replaced. You know?"

"Right," he mumbled, his head swimming from the effort of trying to understand that viewpoint on life. "Uhhhh...ready to go on that tour? My brothers will be here in a couple of hours, so we should probably get going."

As they walked towards the front door together, Stetson turned her words over and over in his mind. A car *was* just a thing that could be replaced. She was right. It just felt...weird.

He'd been raised by a father who emphasized holding onto anything and everything, because as a farmer, he just might need it someday. Stetson liked to pretend that he hadn't been raised to be a hoarder, but really, the only difference between him and a cat lady who owned 102 cats and had her living room stuffed to the ceiling with old newspapers was that his animals were cows instead of cats, and he stuffed his barn full of shit, not his living room.

Ever since he was knee high to a grasshopper, he'd been taught that stuff was important. Stuff had value. If Stetson had broken a piece of farm equipment like he'd just torn off Jennifer's bumper, his father would've been livid. Stetson would've gotten the whaling of his life, and wouldn't have been able to walk for a week.

As alien as Jennifer's viewpoint on life was, Stetson couldn't help thinking that it was more rational. Evenhanded. Focused on what truly mattered in life.

Weird.

CHAPTER 30

JENNIFER

*T*HEY STEPPED off the front porch and into the bright sunshine. She raised her hand up to shield her eyes. She'd been squirreled away in the office for so long, she'd rather forgotten what it was like to go outside into the sunshine and fresh air. It was still cool, the clouds busily scuttling away in the brilliant blue sky, but she knew by tomorrow, it would be hot again – typical summer temperatures. This reprieve from the heat wouldn't last much longer.

Stetson looked down at her skirt and then up at her. "I guess we'll go in the truck. I'd been thinking the four-wheeler, but I don't think you could straddle it in that outfit."

She looked down at the skirt with chagrin. "I wish I'd thought to pack pants," she said, as he helped her swing up into the passenger seat of the truck. "Is there a place in town that sells jeans?"

He closed the door and walked around to the

other side, waiting until he opened the driver's door to answer, "Frank's does. Have you been there yet?"

She wrinkled her nose. "Yeah, I met the tortaco already."

"The *what*?" He started the diesel engine and then turned in his seat to stare at her. "Two taco?"

"No, tortaco. Let's just say that you should thank God every day for Carmelita. Otherwise, you'd know just what I'm talking about."

He chuckled. "Don't let Carma hear you say that. She tells me that often enough."

"I'm sure she does." Jennifer sent him a sassy grin. "Smart woman."

"She tells me that too," he said dryly.

Jennifer snorted with laughter, then turned serious. "What would you think about taking me to town, instead? If I bought jeans and boots and stuff, then tomorrow, you could take me on a proper tour of the farm."

She bit her lip as soon as she said it, her stomach flipping at her audacity. Why would he want to take her clothes shopping? He probably didn't even want to take her on this tour of the farm. He'd probably just offered out of some weird sense of noblesse, like something that he should offer to every guest of the Miller Farm.

"That's a great idea!" he said, shooting her a wide grin. "I really think you'd get a better feel for the place if we could ride around in the four-wheeler anyway."

"Awesome," she said, letting out the breath she'd been holding without realizing it. She opened the door back up again and slid out onto the ground, turning back and looking waaaayyyyy up at Stetson who was still behind the wheel of the truck. "Let me go get my purse. I hadn't expected to need to buy anything on our tour. Be right back!" She shut the door and hurried back up the front steps and into the house. Heart thumping double time, she grabbed her stuff and ran as fast as her skirt and heels would let her back out to the waiting truck.

Either she was sadly out of shape, or just the thought of spending time with Stetson was making her heart go triple time.

Maybe it was both.

That was an idea she was going to ignore, at least for now.

He was waiting for her on the passenger side of the truck so he could help her back in, and then hurried over to his side. As he shifted into gear and headed back towards town, he said, "I was just thinking while you were grabbing your purse...you should probably stay out at the house. You don't have a car to drive back and forth from town, and there's no car rental agency here. You'd have to go over to Franklin or back to Boise to find a rental car to drive, and I just don't see the point. To be honest, Carmelita loves having someone else to hover over besides me. She used to have the whole Miller family to take care of, so just me by myself is boring the hell out of her.

I'm expecting her to adopt a herd of cats any day now, just to have something to do."

Jennifer turned in the passenger seat to stare at Stetson openly. "Where is Mr. This-is-Not-a-Guest-House and what have you done with him?"

The tips of his ears grew red. "I...yeah," he mumbled. "I shouldn't have...your arrival was not something I'd exactly been looking forward to." He grimaced in her general direction. "I was kind of a jackass when you showed up."

Which, Stetson being of the male variety, meant that was as good of an apology as she was going to get. She nodded her acceptance. "Well, I'm thrilled with the idea if you're okay with it. I normally don't stay with clients, but Carmelita's cooking is loads better than anything I can find in town, and the guest room you have me staying in is adorable. I've never seen anything like it in real life. Those roses on the wall – are they hand painted?"

He nodded, a smile of pride spreading across his face, his shoulders easing now that the embarrassment of almost having to say sorry had passed. "My grandma painted those. I never met her...she died in childbirth with my dad. But she had a creative streak a mile wide, and apparently got the hankering to paint that bedroom one day. She wasn't one to slap a coat of white paint on something, though, and before long, there were roses everywhere. My mom always said that she wanted a girl so someone else could appreciate those roses the way she did, but I was their last hope of that happening, and…well, I'm not a girl."

She burst out laughing, taking in his rugged, stubble-covered jaw and muscles flexing under the worn fabric of his jeans. "I wasn't too worried on that topic, but I'm glad to know for sure."

"Disappointing females since 1990 — that's my motto in life."

"I'm sure your mom was glad to have you," Jennifer protested politely.

Stetson shrugged. "My mom was happy, sure, although she would've been happier if I'd been a girl. But my dad…he was thrilled. He told me a few times that he'd screwed up with Wyatt and Declan — didn't do things the way he wanted. He felt like he'd been given a chance to fix those mistakes with me. I honestly think that's why he let me get cows — he never would've let Wyatt or Dec. He would've told them no, absolutely not. But with me, he was trying to be more liberal and open minded. It drives Wyatt and Declan completely mad, by the way. They say I got away with murder compared to them." Stetson shrugged. "They're probably right, although I don't see as how that's *my* fault. Well, we're here!"

Startled, Jennifer looked out the front windshield to see that they were parked in front of Frank's Feed and Fuel. "Oh wow!" she yelped. "How did we… man, I was *not* paying attention to where we were going." A truck ride with Stetson made the minutes just fly by. He could've been driving her to Canada, for all of the attention she'd paid to where they were going and what they were doing.

A little terrifying, that.

Stetson jumped out and hurried around to help her down. Sure, the skirt did make it difficult to maneuver, but she'd been able to get out of the truck back at the farm to fetch her purse all by herself. His help wasn't strictly necessary, even if the truck was as oversized as Stetson was.

As he swung her out of the cab and down to the ground, though, his hands lightly clasped around her waist, she got the impression that Stetson enjoyed helping her out of the truck a little more than he might've enjoyed helping a little old lady. The thought made the back of her neck tingle and she grinned to herself. Yeah, she might be wrong, but somehow, she was *quite* sure she wasn't.

All of which was weird, of course. She'd spent three years with Paul, who'd made sure to tell her in great detail just how undesirable she was. Having Stetson look at her with something other than pity and disgust…

It was making her head hurt somethin' fierce.

She moved forward to grab her purse off the passenger-side floor of the truck when she brushed up against one very hard, very aroused Stetson. She shouldn't have reacted – somewhere deep inside of her she knew that – but she couldn't help herself. It was instinctual – she let out a little gasp and her eyes flew up to his to find he was staring down at her, naked hunger blazing in their depths.

"I shouldn't, I know I shouldn't…but I can't help myself," he murmured, cupping her face in his hand and swiping the pad of his thumb across her lips. She trembled, need pouring through her. If they weren't standing on Main Street in town, she'd be launching herself at him at that very moment.

"I…I can't help myself either," she whispered back, her tongue flicking out and swiping across the calloused end of his thumb. His eyes went darker still and he pulled in a hiss of air.

"Let's go shopping, shall we?" he murmured, his voice hoarse with need. "Then we can stop by the motel to get your stuff, then head back to the farm."

The promise was obvious, if unspoken, about *exactly* what would happen once they got back to the farm.

Jennifer wasn't sure she'd live through the wait.

CHAPTER 31

STETSON

*T*HEY PULLED UP in front of the house, and Stetson hurried around to help her out of the truck, eager to put his hands back on her body, even if he was excusing it by using the cover of politeness to get away with it. Anything to put his hands on her body – anything at all, at this point. Watching her come out of the dressing room at Frank's in Wranglers, her ass shown off to perfection...

He held up his arms and she willingly moved into them. He swung her down to the ground, as surprised the second time as he had been the first. She was so light – like picking up a hay bale or a newborn calf. How was it that she could be a full-grown woman?

Or *was* she?

He stared down at her in horror for a moment, finally blurting out, "How old are you?" He had terrifying visions dancing through his head of finding out that she was actually fifteen years old and just some sort of accountant prodigy.

"I'm 24. Why?"

"Oh my God!" he exclaimed, relief and shock pouring through him. "You're only two years younger than me. How is that possible?"

"I'm going to guess that my mother gave birth two years after your mother did," Jennifer said dryly.

"But you're so small," he protested. "And short. And not at all tall."

It was at this point that he decided that talking to Jennifer Kendall was just God's way of keeping him humble. He was apparently completely incapable of speaking coherently around her.

"It's possible – just possible – that *my* father isn't cousin to Godzilla," she retorted. "It isn't my fault all of the men in Sawyer are giants." She crossed her arms and stared up at him defiantly, her green eyes flashing.

Shit.

He decided that rather than try to extract his size 17 boot from his mouth – which was probably an impossible task at this point anyway – he'd just sidetrack her. With any luck, she'd forget all about this conversation.

Just to show he could, he scooped her up into his arms and started carrying her towards the farmhouse, ignoring her squeal of protests, mostly centering on the fact that they were leaving her bags behind.

Whatever. They could fetch her clothes later. What he had in mind did not involve clothing.

He looked up when he heard a little howl of delight, and with panic spreading through him, he saw Maggie Mae headed straight towards them, tail going a million miles a minute.

Dammit. If Maggie was here, Wyatt was here.

Sure enough, he looked up past his brother's mutt of a dog to see both of his brother's trucks parked outside of the barn. He let a string of curses out that was likely to set the prairie grass on fire.

"What? What is it?" Jennifer was craning her neck around, clearly not understanding the importance of the two trucks parked side by side by the barn's sliding door.

"I...forgot." For a couple of hours, he'd let himself forget about the meeting with his brothers, and the arguments sure to come along with it. A few glorious hours without worry that he was loathe to leave behind. He wanted to spin on his boot heel and head back to the truck to drive anywhere but there – leave it all behind – but skipping out on the meeting would only make things worse.

If that was even possible at this point.

"Wyatt and Declan are here. Hence Maggie." He let Jennifer slide down his front in a deliciously painful descent to the ground, nearly groaning at the pleasure it brought him. "Meet Maggie Mae. Maggie Mae, this is Jennifer."

Maggie, a loyal, hardworking, sweetheart of a dog

160 | ERIN WRIGHT

that Wyatt absolutely did not deserve whatsoever, busily set about licking Jennifer's hand, her tail wagging madly with pleasure when Jennifer used her other hand to scratch behind her ears. "Oh, aren't you a sweetie," Jennifer crooned.

Stetson was trying pretty damn hard not to be jealous of Wyatt's dog just then, which was ridiculous, even to him.

"I need to go meet up with my brothers," he said with a jerk of his head towards the barn. "I'll…be back in a little while."

It was an awkward-as-hell goodbye, because he wanted to kiss her but they weren't exactly at the casual-kiss-goodbye point in their relationship but not doing something also felt weird and he thought about hugging her but she was still bent over, petting Maggie, who had obligingly rolled over onto her back so she could get belly rubs, so hugging Jennifer was weird too, so he settled for tugging on the brim of his Stetson and heading for the barn.

Girls were so confusing sometimes.

He walked into the barn, the massive sliding door already open from his brothers making their way in.

I can do this. I can totally do this. I will not beat Wyatt into the ground. We will make Dad proud.

He found his brothers sitting on a couple of crates, bullshitting quietly to each other as they waited for him to show up. Stetson bit back his groan. Being late was *not* going to help matters.

"Hey," he said casually, jerking his head in

greeting as he leaned on the bumper of one of the work trucks. Usually, Declan had the schedule worked out, so Stetson waited quietly for him to begin.

"'Bout damn time you showed up," Wyatt snarled. Stetson just cocked an eyebrow at him and stayed silent. If Wyatt thought he was going to apologize to him, he was going to be sorely disappointed.

"Let's just get going," Declan put in, ever the peacemaker. Stetson rolled his eyes. Someday, Declan would grow a backbone and tell Wyatt to stop being a jackass. Until then, it was hard to take the guy seriously, even if he was Stetson's favorite brother.

Not exactly the most difficult contest in the world to win.

"So, here's the deal," Wyatt said, begrudgingly taking Declan's advice. "It's been a downright awful year for water, other than this shitload of rain that we just had, so my dryland wheat is ripening real quick. It's gonna need to be harvested before it rots on the stem. Stetson, you bring the trucks up next week. You still have three guys, right?"

"Yeah, I've got three right now," Stetson said, trying to ignore the fact that Wyatt had just ordered him to bring the trucks over next week instead of asking. If he was going to start getting pissy over small details like that, he and Wyatt would never be able to hold a conversation again. "When you thinkin' of starting? I haven't done the oil changes on the trucks yet."

"We're starting Monday," Wyatt said flatly.

"I can't do that!" Stetson protested. "I gave the guys the weekend off; told 'em to enjoy their last weekend of freedom since harvest was about to begin. I can't start until Tuesday or maybe Wednesday."

"Dammit, Stetson, do we always have to hold your hand?" Wyatt snapped.

"My trucks aren't ready either," Declan jumped in, trying to placate them. Stetson and Wyatt both ignored him.

"I don't get it," Stetson growled. "Unless the wind picks up and dries your wheat out, your harvest is gonna be shit anyway. Why not just call up your crop insurance agent and collect a payout for this year? Getting trucks into the field is gonna be rough on 'em – we're gonna spend half our time pulling machines out of the mud, and then turning around and getting them stuck again. For hell's sakes, just call it for the year."

"I am not going to collect insurance on my wheat! Some of us have to work for what we get, and not just get it handed to us for twiddling our thumbs."

That was a direct hit, and everyone knew it. Time slowed down as Stetson froze in place, staring at his oldest brother, pure anger boiling through his veins. "You *bastard!*" he roared, his fists clenched at his side. "*I* was the one who took care of Dad and paid for his chemo treatments. I noticed you were nowhere to be found for that part of it."

"Some of us had already grown up and bought our own farms," Wyatt volleyed back smugly. "If I'd been able to just sit around and wait to have everything handed to me, I could've played Dad's nursemaid too, but I had a bank loan to pay."

"What, and I didn't?" Stetson shot back. "Dad had an operating loan every year. Has for years. You know that. Just because I got the farm doesn't mean I inherited it free and clear."

"Oh, so is that why you've hired a bookkeeper to run your adding machine for you?" Wyatt demanded. "Incapable of adding a few numbers up by yourself?"

"It's a good thing that Stetson hired someone to help him out," Declan put in, trying to simmer things down a notch. Again, Stetson and Wyatt both ignored him.

"She ain't a bookkeeper," Stetson said flatly. He didn't want to tell his brothers – especially not right now – but lying didn't sit right on his soul. It was time to come clean, and deal with the aftermath.

"What?!" Declan hollered, getting angry himself for the first time. "You told me you'd hired a bookkeeper to go over things—"

"I know what I said," Stetson cut him off, still not looking at him. His eyes were locked on Wyatt who was glaring back at him, anger radiating off him in waves. It was a pretty fair bet that Wyatt would never forgive him for what he was about to say.

It was also a pretty fair bet that Stetson didn't care.

"It's the bank. Intermountain. There was a balloon payment on that loan that was due on

January 1st, and I didn't make it." Stetson was talking quickly now, keeping Wyatt from interrupting him. "The accountant is here on behalf of Intermountain, to see if there's a way for me to make that payment."

"Holy *shit!*" Wyatt exploded. "I can't believe it! I was right. You idiot! I bet it was those stupid cows sucking down all of the money."

"Hold on a moment here – Dad's cancer took all the money from the cows. I noticed you couldn't be bothered to contribute to that effort. It was *my* cows that gave Dad an extra six months," Stetson spat out.

"Why didn't you tell me?" Declan asked, clearly hurt by Stetson's silence. "We would've helped you."

"Oh yeah, rain more money down on the *Golden Boy* so he doesn't have to learn how to work," Wyatt threw out sarcastically at Declan, even as he advanced on Stetson. "*I* should pay off the loan and take over the farm," he said, jabbing himself in the chest with his thumb. "It should've been me that got it anyway! I'm the oldest."

"Hear ye, hear ye, the perfect brother who has never had any problems," Stetson said with a heaping dose of his own sarcasm. "Please, do tell me how to farm. I'd love to hear *all* about it."

"You need me to tell you how, 'cause it's so hard having everything handed to you on a silver platter. Grow up, you whiny little bastard," Wyatt bellowed, his spittle hitting Stetson's cheeks. They were so close, Stetson could see the red veins in his brother's eyes, popping as he yelled. "Don't you ever think that your bedwetting problems are anything close to what I've had to live through. I am ten times the man you will ever dream to be. No wonder Michelle left you standing in the church. No woman wants to marry a baby."

The comment hit well below the belt. Past caring, past stopping, past reason, Stetson saw red as he went in for the verbal blow.

"You're a real man, all right." Stetson's voice was low and full of danger. "You've been directing your anger at us for so long, I sometimes wonder if you've bothered to get around to being pissed at the drunk driver who actually killed your wife and daughter. Stop blaming us for what happened."

Stetson knew he was pressing Wyatt's biggest button with a sledgehammer but he couldn't bring himself to care.

The words were barely out before Wyatt launched himself at his youngest brother.

Stetson was ready. The brothers collided like a train running into a mountainside. They tumbled to the ground, fists flying as they fell. The two angry men rolled around on the dusty barn floor, each blinded by rage. Some blows missed while others found their mark.

Somewhere in the distance, they could hear Declan yelling for them to stop, but neither paid him any mind. The air was split with the sounds of fists striking flesh. Blows were punctuated with a litany of swear words.

For the first time in their lives, Stetson gained the upper hand in a fight. Pinning Wyatt to the ground with his knees, Stetson's fist connected with his brother's cheek. Wyatt's lip split as his face contorted from the punch.

The single blow was almost victory enough for Stetson. Almost.

Cocking his arm back, Stetson readied to strike again if Wyatt pushed the issue.

"You can harvest your damn grain without my help," Stetson growled. "Now get the hell off my farm." He rolled off Wyatt and onto his feet in one smooth motion.

Dusting himself off as he stood up, Wyatt glowered at Stetson for a long, considering moment before he spat blood on the floor and stormed out of the barn, Maggie Mae following behind, tail tucked between her legs.

Declan and Stetson shared an awkward moment before Declan shrugged and followed Wyatt.

"We'll talk later," Declan said, before pulling the massive door shut behind him.

"I SWEAR, every time you go out to the barn, you come back bleeding. I'm not going to allow you to continue to go out there if this keeps up," Jennifer joked as she dabbed at the cut over his left eye.

Wyatt had managed to land one really good punch during their tussle in the barn, damn him.

Stetson was feeling bad, but not because of the fight. He was actually feeling pretty good about that. Well, at least the part where he'd come out on top in a fistfight with Wyatt. That had never happened before, so yeah, that part felt good. Awfully damn good, if he was being honest with himself. Even if he'd had to punch Wyatt with his knuckles that he'd already hurt working on the tractor, he didn't care.

But his jab about Shelly and Sierra dying – that wasn't his finest hour. Now, just minutes later, he was already starting to regret saying it. If Wyatt wasn't such a dick, he'd totally apologize to him for it.

Too bad Wyatt was a class-A dickwad.

No, what Stetson was *really* feeling bad about was that he'd ruined Jennifer's mood when he'd walked in the door with blood streaming down his face. She'd bounded out of the office when she'd heard the back door open but her happiness had vanished when she'd caught sight of him.

She'd dragged him into the kitchen and plopped him down at the kitchen table, giving her the height advantage for once, and then had proceeded to dote on him. Stetson had visions of having to turn a corner of the kitchen into a first aid station if the injuries continued.

"So what happened?" she asked gently as she dabbed at his eye.

"Oh, you know how brothers are," he answered, hoping to downplay what had happened. Actually, he preferred not to discuss it at all. Females didn't tend to understand the intricacies of male relationships.

"I'm an only child, so no, I don't know about brothers," she murmured, peering closely at the cut. "This might need stitches…"

"We show each other our love by wanting to kill each other," Stetson said, ignoring the stitches comment. He'd heal without stitches. He had before. "It's complicated."

"Sounds like a dangerous relationship."

"It usually is," Stetson agreed blandly. "Where's Carmelita?"

"I think she's changing bedding or something," Jennifer murmured. She was bent over, her button-up pearl snap shirt falling away from her chest as she looked closely at his eye. Stetson enjoyed the view, forgetting for a moment how to breathe. If she didn't remove that delectable chest out of reach real quick, he was gonna pop a button on his jeans.

Or simply grab her and make love to her on the kitchen table.

His impulse control wasn't real high today.

"Well," she said, thankfully – or horribly, depending on how you looked at it – straightening up and putting her hands on her hips, "it's right on the border. We could try and see if we could get away without using stitches on it. We need to get the bleeding to stop, and then I'll use some Krazy Glue to seal it up."

"Hold on, you're going to glue my head back together?" Suddenly, the idea of stitches didn't seem so bad after all.

"That's what a hospital uses when you go in with a cut," she said with a shrug, washing her hands in the kitchen sink. "They use a fancier name for it, but it's basically super glue. If the cut isn't too severe, it works much better than stitches. Heals a lot faster, with less pain."

"Sometimes you medical people are sure weird,"

Stetson grumbled, holding the cotton gauze up to his eye that Jennifer had forced into his hand.

"Hey, I'm not the one who just got in a fistfight with my brother." She grinned teasingly at him, and Stetson felt himself smiling back.

Smiling. After he and Wyatt had rolled around on the barn floor, beating the hell out of each other, Stetson found himself *smiling*.

Wasn't that just the damnedest thing.

CHAPTER 33

JENNIFER

*D*INNER WAS turning out to be a rather quiet affair. When Carmelita had come back downstairs, her arms full of laundry, she'd taken one look at Stetson's eye and launched into him for daring to fight with Wyatt. Jennifer couldn't help noticing that Carmelita had just assumed that the fight was with Wyatt, without even asking any questions first.

Smart woman.

Stetson had taken it all like a small child, only occasionally trying to interrupt and defend himself, but quickly realizing the futility of it and falling silent again.

Eyes bouncing between them like a spectator at a tennis match, Jennifer was pretty damn sure that this was a "discussion" the two of them had had more than once.

Hmmm...I definitely need to meet these brothers of

Stetson's. See why they're so difficult to get along with. Or at least why Wyatt is.

Once the scolding was done, Carma had led them into the dining room where she'd laid out a stunning dinner for them – lasagna, tossed salad fresh from the garden, and homemade garlic bread. She then had disappeared, murmuring something about chores she needed to do. Jennifer had stared after her. "Is she always that obvious?" she'd asked dryly.

"Pretty much!" Stetson had said cheerfully.

That had been the last of their conversation for quite a while, actually. Jennifer wasn't sure if it was because the food was so amazing, there was no time for talking, or if Stetson just didn't have anything to say to her.

Finally, he spoke up. "You never told me why you became an accountant," he said, piling a third helping of lasagna onto his plate. How could he eat so much and still stay in such good shape? The Miller genes at work were a sight to behold.

"I didn't?" she asked, confused. She thought they'd already discussed all of this.

"Nope. You told me why you quit the nursing profession, but you didn't tell me why you then chose to become an accountant. It's not like that's a given or something – if you don't like the medical field, you automatically become an accountant."

"Oh. Yeah. No, you're right. I guess that does seem like a strange switch, from the outside. It made perfect sense to me, but then again, your own actions usually do." She took another sip of her wine, letting the warmth spread through her. "I'd gotten into the nursing profession because I wanted to help people. I figured out that I don't like poop and blood all that much, but I still like to help people, so I decided that I could do it by becoming an accountant."

"Stealing people's farms away from them is helping them?" Stetson cocked an eyebrow at her in disbelief.

She glared at him. "I don't go around holding a gun to people's heads and taking their stuff from them, first of all," she informed him tartly. "They have to have missed payments with the bank, which is *not* my fault. Second, like I said, working for Intermountain in the audit department wasn't really my dream job, or the reason I went to school to become an accountant. They were just the ones hiring when I graduated from Boise State, and I have a crapload of student loans I need to pay off. Beggars can't be choosers."

They stared at each other for a long minute as Stetson chewed his lasagna in silence, his face a wall of stone. No emotion leaked through as his jaw moved rhythmically, eyes locked together in a silent struggle.

Finally, he swallowed and then nodded. Just once. "You're right," he said gruffly, looking down at his plate as he spoke. "I've been looking at Intermountain as the enemy for so long, it's rough...I don't change my views with a snap of the fingers. But..." He heaved a huge sigh and looked up at her, his cheeks tinged a little red. "I...I did miss the payment. That $176,000 is the bank's money, not mine. No matter how I got into this mess, a man still pays his bills."

Jennifer was sure that the pain Stetson had just endured from having to swallow his pride like a piece of jagged glass was probably sharp and cutting and terrible. Although he didn't say the exact words "I'm sorry," they were implied, and she already knew him well enough to know just that alone was a mighty big step for him.

She nodded, deliberately choosing to let it go and move on. She wouldn't win any brownie points by pushing the topic further, and an implied apology was almost as good as a stated one.

Almost.

"To answer your question," she said, going back to the start of the conversation, "I wanted to become an accountant because I wanted to help people, plus I'm fairly good with numbers and organizing stuff. I may not like blood or poop, but I do like spreadsheets and numbers. It's logical – something that I can quantify.

"You haven't met her, of course, but Bonnie Patterson is my best friend. We met in an accounting class at Boise State and we quickly became best friends because we both look at the world in the same way. We realized when we met that we were both getting into accounting for the same reason: So we could help small business owners with their books and taxes. Most normal people don't run a business because they love pushing paper around. You may or may not have some experience in this arena." He flashed her a grin at her quip and she pushed herself to smile back, a smile tinged with sadness and frustration.

"But instead of being able to help small business owners, we've both ended up at jobs that we hate, working for people we despise. It's kind of depressing how different our careers ended up being, compared to what we'd wanted to do. It's hard to stay optimistic when the whole reason for your career choice ends up being not at all what happens in that career."

She shrugged and took another sip of her wine. She looked up at Stetson and said with a forced cheerfulness, "Well, enough of that. No one wants to focus on the negative, right?"

He ignored her horribly blatant attempt at changing the subject, and instead said softly, "I don't know how you stay so cheerful all the time. You said earlier that it's not hard to stay optimistic when so much of your life has gone your way, but honestly Jenn, it seems like so much of it hasn't."

She opened up her mouth to protest, and then closed it again with a snap. She stared at him. He stared back.

Finally, she sputtered, "Well, sure, if you focus on all of the bad things that have happened, life sucks, but you know, I've had lots of wonderful things happen too." She began listing them off on her fingers. "I was able to graduate from high school a year early by taking accelerated and summer classes, which meant I could get a head start on my secondary education. I have very supportive parents, even if they're a bit overbearing at times. I realized quicker than most that I needed a career change, instead of wallowing in frustration and misery for decades. I met Bonnie while going to BSU for the second time, and we ended up being roommates for years. She's like a sister I never got to have, and if I'd gone straight from high school to college and studied accounting straight out of the gate, we probably never would've met. So in some ways, I have Paul to thank for meeting Bonnie."

Stetson shook his head, a small smile dancing around his lips. "You are the very embodiment of making lemonade out of lemons. If I had half your optimism and happiness, I probably wouldn't have punched Wyatt today. You...you're like this alien being come to earth. I've never met anyone like you."

"Alien being?!" Jennifer repeated with a snort of laughter. "Hey Romeo, anyone ever told you that you need to work on your pickup lines?"

"I've never had any complaints before," he said with a grin and a wink that ended with a groan. He reached up to touch his eye tentatively.

"I think your first clue should've been the fact that you're 26 and single," she pointed out, ignoring his grunt of pain. Maybe next time he'd think twice before getting into a fistfight with his own damn brother.

"Hey, you're 24 and single!" he protested, his cheeks heating up.

"Which is waaayyyy younger than 26." She grinned at him, which was when he realized that she'd been teasing him.

"Damn you," he growled. "Come here. I'll teach you to be nice to your elders." He reached over and snagged her arm, pulling her onto his lap. She laughed up into his face.

"Elder, eh? I guess it's progress that you at least recognize that part."

Which was when he swooped down onto her mouth and began plundering it with his tongue. All laughter quickly died away and she kissed him back, moaning with pleasure as she did so. All day, she'd been waiting for this moment, hoping against hope that he'd see past all of her flaws and still want her.

And somehow, he did.

For Jennifer, the kiss was straight out of a fairytale. She felt lightheaded from the excitement and the wine as the world narrowed to just the two of them. She focused on the point where their lips met, relishing the sensation of his tongue pushing at her lips. A chorus in her mind cheered when she relented, opening her mouth. Everything in her celebrated that brief moment where nothing else in the world mattered.

Slowly, languidly, she pulled back and opened her eyes, her hand drifting lightly over his chest while

Stetson's hand slid down her back. She felt his palm fall slightly into the hollow of her back before it settled on the curve of her ass. The pressure of his hand was perfect. Firm and demanding, but not so insistent as to be controlling.

He brought his other hand up to her face. He rested his palm on her cheek and his long fingers, rough against her soft skin, curled just a bit around the back of her head. His eyes burned through her for just the briefest of moments before he bent and pulled her in for a second kiss.

Jennifer let him explore her mouth with his tongue again before pressing her tongue back against his. She reveled in the newness of this man's body. In response to what was happening, her body began to radiate a rhythmic warmth in time with her pounding pulse.

He pulled away suddenly. The abrupt end shocked her. Her eyes shot open, and she looked up at him in confusion. She saw nothing but fire.

"Come with me," was all he said, his voice husky and breathless. His obvious desire was contagious and undeniable. She nodded her head, unable to speak. Stetson pulled her through the house and up the stairs to the bedroom, his impatience rolling off him in waves. Walking to the end of the massive bed that was centered in the room, Stetson turned to face the trailing Jennifer.

She took in the room in a theoretical sense – she saw dark cherry wood dressers and nightstands and a bed frame that all matched, a rug at the foot of the bed to warm up the wood floors – but it was a hazy kind of awareness that only served to keep her from bumping into the dresser as she walked towards him. At gunpoint, she wouldn't have been able to say if there was a single painting or mirror on any of the walls.

All that existed was Stetson.

He smiled. She'd really liked his smile earlier in the day, but she *loved* this smile. There was something sinfully fun promised in this smile.

He grabbed the edges of her shirt and pulled, the pearl-snap buttons popping their release up her front. She was starting to realize the benefits that came from snap buttons – maybe country folk were onto something.

But even as she felt lust and desire begin to thrum through her veins, panic started to seep in around the edges. It was just about to get bad. Maybe she could hurry him along through the bad part and he could still want to have sex with her.

It was totally possible, right?

Stetson sat down on the end of the bed, giving her the height advantage for once. It was rather nice, actually. He reached around her and unsnapped her lacy bra, letting the light-as-air fabric fall to the floor. When someone was as small as she was, they didn't need much in the way of boob support, dammit.

She instinctively covered her chest with her hands – her tiny boobs were probably why he'd demanded earlier that day to know how old she was. He'd likely thought she was still a child. She got that response sometimes when meeting men for the first time.

Well, if she could just cover her tits from his gaze, maybe he wouldn't notice how tiny they were and be turned off by them. God only knew how many times she'd heard from Paul about how she wasn't large enough to really make a man happy. She didn't need to hear it from anyone else.

He slowly peeled her fingers off her chest, one by one, kissing each finger until she was laid bare to his gaze. She trembled a little, moaning in distress. This was when it'd start – the derogatory comments. The obvious statements about not being woman enough for a *real* man.

"So perfect. So beautiful," he whispered and then he leaned forward and suckled on one nipple and then the other as she stared down at his lighter locks on top in shock. He couldn't mean it. Why, she looked like she'd been bitten by mosquitoes! That wasn't sexy. It was okay if he ignored her breasts and moved on to the good stuff, but he shouldn't try to bullshit her so blatantly.

Panic and anger were overwhelming her, washing over her, drowning her in their wake.

Why was he lying to her?

"Don't lie!" she shouted, pushing at his shoulders, shoving him away from her. It was probably the shock of it that allowed her pushing at him to actually move him. He hadn't been expecting it.

Good.

She covered her tits again with her hands as she glared down at him. His eyes were wide as he stared back.

"Wha–what?" he stuttered.

"Don't lie to me. They're not perfect or beautiful. They're tiny – a child's size. They're not even worth looking at!" She spat out Paul's favorite criticism of them before Stetson could say it first. It hurt less if she was the one to say it – she'd figured that out a long time ago.

"Are you...who told you that?" he demanded, peeling her fingers away again, but this time, Jennifer twisted out of his grasp.

"I knew this was a bad idea," she mumbled as she began gathering up her clothes. "Stupid, ugly Jennifer."

Then she was being lifted in the air and swung around to the bed, where Stetson plopped her down.

"You—" she yelled, starting to scramble off the bed.

He threw himself on top of her and pinned her in place. She struggled and pushed and squirmed, but it was like a granite block had landed on top of her – not squishing her flat, but she wasn't going anywhere until he was willing to let her. Finally, worn out, she slowed to a stop. "Why are you keeping me here?" she asked dully, staring up over his shoulder at the ceiling. "Do you want to force me to listen to all of the ways that I'm failing you? I've lived through that before. Don't think you'll come up with something new."

"Who the hell did this—whoa. Whoa. Okay." He took in a few deep breaths and blew them back out again. "Paul — was it Paul who said those things to you?"

She shrugged — moving as much of her shoulders as Stetson would allow anyway — and continued to stare up at the ceiling. There was a swirl in the plaster that looked like a cloud scuttling across the ceiling. She focused on it. It was safe. Just a cloud moving on the breeze — free to go where it wanted; do what it wanted.

"Jennifer, I do think you're perfect and beautiful. Your breasts are just the right size, and come equipped with the most exquisite pink tips that I want to lick like ice cream."

"Like ice cream!" she repeated, her eyes jerking from the plaster cloud to his. "But how could you like—"

"Babe, I don't know if anyone's ever told you this, but guys tend to fixate on female body parts. Like, some guys are tits guys, and some guys are ass guys, and some guys are all about the legs, you know? Not every woman has to look like a replica of a Barbie doll for hell's sakes. Me? I like the trim, sleek look and for the record, I'm a total ass and legs guy. I mean, tits are fun and I meant what I said about wanting to lick yours like ice cream, but have you ever stared at your legs in the mirror? Or your ass?"

She shook her head tremulously, not trusting herself to speak. Was he lying? If he was, he was the world's best liar. He seemed to mean every word he said.

Which she just wasn't even sure how to process.

"Well, you should. Although I don't suppose that you'd find them nearly as sexy as I find them, since we humans always seem to focus on our flaws instead of our good parts. Me, for example. There's this scar right here." He pointed to a light scar at his temple that she hadn't even noticed before. "A horse kicked me when I got too close to his back legs. I was a kid and playing around where I shouldn't have been. My dad didn't notice until it was too late. The horse's kick knocked me clean out, and I had to have seven stitches to close up the gash. Dad always joked that my hard head saved my life that day. The truth of the matter is, I'm not so sure that it's a joke."

"But I hadn't even noticed that scar before," she protested. "It's such a tiny thing. My boobs…well, they're tiny too, but not in a good way." She wanted to cross her arms across her chest again, but Stetson wasn't letting her move.

"I guess I'm just going to have to prove to you how delicious you look to me," he said softly, and then bent down and began nibbling at her tits, licking and sucking and lightly biting his way across one and then the other. After he swirled his tongue over each peak, groaning with pleasure as he did, he blew a stream of cold air across them, causing them to tighten up and almost reach straight for his mouth.

Traitors. They didn't seem to know that they were

playing with fire; that trusting a man was a scary thing to do.

He grinned cockily up at her. "I do believe that I've at least convinced part of your body to believe me, even if I haven't convinced the most important part yet."

"Most important part?" she repeated faintly, realizing that a part of her wanted him to just get back to bathing her nipples in kisses, which was *not* a thought she ever believed she'd have.

"Your brain. But I'll convince it someday."

And with that, he went back to lavishing her nipples with his tongue, and then began working his way down her stomach and tiny waist – finally, a feature that she was proud of – until he got to the apex of her thighs.

"I've been smelling this pussy for days, I swear it," he growled, looking up at her with hot eyes. "I've wanted to do nothing more than to bury my nose in it since the day you got here."

"Really?" she panted, surprised. *He likes how I smell…is he lying about that too?* "I…I thought you hated me the day I got here."

"Didn't mean I didn't want a taste of your pussy too," he said, verbally shrugging, and then he got to work, running his tongue up her slit and to her clit, and back down again.

Jenn began to writhe on the bed, pleasure singing through her veins. "Oh, oh, oohhhhhh…" she groaned, shoving her fingers into his hair and holding on tight.

He pulled the lips of her pussy gently to the sides, and then blew lightly across the wet, hyper-sensitive flesh. "Oooohhhhhhhhh!" she howled, digging her fingers tighter into his hair. "Yes, oh please, oh yesssss..." she hissed as he continued to kiss and lick and blow. He brought her closer and closer to the precipice with every flick of his tongue, until she was plunging over the side and howling with delight, her thighs clasping his head and riding his tongue.

Finally, he pulled away, her juices practically dripping off his chin, and grinned at her triumphantly. "You make me feel like a million bucks, you know that?" he said, worming his way back up her side until he was hovering over her again.

She smiled dreamily up at him. "I make you feel like a million bucks?" she said, laughing quietly. "Do you know what you just did to me?"

"That's why you make me feel like a million bucks. Truthfully, you're the most gorgeous woman I've ever been in bed with. I can't begin to figure out why on God's green earth you agreed to this. But honestly, it doesn't really matter how gorgeous a woman is; if she's enthusiastic and loving in bed, she's going to be amazing. If she's gorgeous but bored and demanding in bed, she's gonna be as ugly as a toad. Women don't seem to understand how much power they hold in their little pinky."

The laughter on her lips died and she just stared at him for the longest time. He gave her the mental and physical space to think through what he just said, and the small part of her brain not occupied with wrestling this new viewpoint into submission, appreciated that breathing room.

"I didn't know," she finally said softly. "It…it makes sense. I guess. My whole life, I thought guys only cared about looks. I mean, have you picked up a fashion magazine lately? Or watched a TV show? Looks have always been what mattered. Nothing else."

He began kissing his way down her side, tickling her with his scruff on his jaw. She writhed on the bed, begging him to stop between her howls of laughter, until he finally looked up and said with a naughty grin, "Oh, looks still matter, and I happen to think you're *gorgeous*. But they only matter for roughly 3.7 seconds after I meet a girl. From there, personality takes over."

"At 3.8 seconds?" she asked, laughing.

"Maybe 3.9," he said solemnly, and then winked. And then groaned.

"Want me to kiss it better?" she asked, teasing him. "When I glued you earlier, I forgot to kiss it when I was done."

"Probably a good idea, really. What if your lips had become glued to my forehead? I think that would've been difficult to explain to Carmelita."

She burst out laughing. "I think Carmelita definitely would've had questions," she said dryly.

"Is it always this much fun to have sex with you?" he asked bluntly.

"What?!" she yelped, caught off guard by the question.

"I don't think I've ever laughed this much in bed before. I was just curious if sex is always like this for you."

Her mind flashed back to the humiliation, the negativity, the assessments of her body, and how she never lived up to the standards of a *real* woman.

"I don't think I've ever laughed in bed before," she said seriously. "I'm trying to remember a time, and… no. I haven't."

His eyes were serious even as he said lightly, "Well, let's start breaking some records together, shall we? Have you ever come twice while having sex with a guy?"

She blew out a startled laugh. "I was lucky if I came once," she said dryly. "Twice…never."

"I think that's something we oughta change," he said with a naughty grin.

And then he set about doing just that.

CHAPTER 34

STETSON

*H*E ROLLED OVER, his nose leading him before his brain could even begin to register anything. There was the most delicious perfume in the air…

And then he was snuggled against something warm and amazingly soft and his eyes popped open. "What the—" he rasped out, before his brain finally caught up with the rest of him.

Oh. Right. He was in bed, like always, but this time, there was a Jennifer Kendall in bed with him.

Which was *not* like always.

Her face was slack and open and trusting, deeply asleep, and he took the opportunity to study her without her blushing or trying to change the subject or, heaven forbid, walking away. Her long, thick eyelashes laid like little miniature fans against her cheeks, hiding the brilliance of the green eyes underneath. He swallowed hard. He was honestly glad to have those hidden from him, at least for the moment. They flustered him so much, it was hard to think when they were trained on him.

Not, of course, that he'd admit that out loud to her. She was brave enough to open up a little to him last night, and he could only admire that bravery, without actually being ready to mimic it himself. He'd opened up to a female before, and even if this one was more beautiful and more happy and more open than the last female, it still didn't mean he could entirely trust her.

Trust was a hard-won thing in his world.

His eyes skimmed over her pert nose and small chin, down to her collarbone, then dipping down to her delicious tits.

He'd meant every word that he'd said the night before, of course – lying to a woman never turned out well, in his experience – and the sight of the pink tips, soft and plump, were hard to ignore. He licked his lips, forcing himself not to lock his mouth around her nipples. She was dead asleep and probably wouldn't appreciate a horny cowboy forcing himself on her first thing in the morning.

He pushed himself out of bed and into the shower. She needed her sleep – he'd quite happily kept her up most of the night – so he'd best get some work done and leave her the hell alone. She could come downstairs when she was ready, and not a minute before.

CHAPTER 35

JENNIFER

*J*ENNIFER JACKKNIFED straight up, her heart tripping into overtime, panic gripping her. She was alone. Why did that scare her? She was always alone. But she shouldn't be alone today. It was wrong, somehow. And she certainly shouldn't be alone in a weird room. Whose room…? She looked wildly around, completely disoriented. Nothing looked familiar. Where was she?

It took her a few seconds to register what she was feeling – she was feeling empty sheets. She'd expected to find a sleeping man next to her and instead she found…nothing.

Oh.

She was in Stetson's room.

By herself.

Stetson had left her.

Not again. Something's wrong. Panic pulsed through her, making it hard to concentrate. *Maybe…maybe it just meant more to me than it did him. I've been through this before. It's going to be okay. It was fun, but this is just one of those things, right?*

She dressed quickly in Stetson's t-shirt and shorts that she'd commandeered as her PJs and headed down the stairs. She had to apologize for her lack of professionalism to both Stetson and Carmelita, keep her head up the whole time, and then get a ride back to town. Maybe Carmelita would drive her. She could re-rent her old room at the Drop-Inn Motel, and just ignore the strange looks that Margaret would give her.

Then she could beat herself up, in the privacy of the dingy motel room.

Don't let him know it hurt. That gives him all the power.

She could totally pretend she was fine. Totally.

When she reached the base of the stairs, she could hear voices drifting through from the kitchen.

"...her that I have some chores to do? I'll be back in a little while. I'm going to take her on a tour of the farm this morning, now that she has some real clothes to wear."

Jennifer paused outside of the doorway to the kitchen, plastering herself up against the hallway wall. She felt ridiculous for hiding from Stetson and Carmelita, but as she listened to them chit-chat and then heard the back door open and close behind Stetson, she felt even more ridiculous for her reaction to waking up alone.

C'mon, Jennifer, think about it. Stetson wouldn't lie to

Carmelita about something like going out to do chores. Of course he has chores to do. He's a farmer, for heaven's sake.

Which made a lot more sense than he was trying to leave her because he didn't think her tits were big enough.

She shoved her hands through her hair and scrubbed at her eyes. Now that her brain was functioning a little better, she could laugh at her lizard-brain reaction to waking up by herself. She wasn't sure what it meant, that that was where her brain leapt to first.

Nothing good, she was sure.

She took a few deep breaths, pushing the panic down. She felt her heart rate slow, and her muscles unclench. She was fine.

A little more relaxed, she put her shoulders back and walked into the kitchen with a big smile planted firmly on her lips, letting out a yawn that she politely hid behind her hand. "Good morning, Carmelita," she said around her yawn.

But now that her first blush of panic had disappeared, she found that a second wave was right on its heels, but this time, it was centered on the housekeeper.

How much did Carmelita know? How much did she guess? This was like trying to sneak around with a boyfriend in high school. She hadn't been good at it in high school, and she had a sinking suspicion she wasn't any better at it now.

For the first time, Jennifer could see a downside to

having a live-in housekeeper – okay, one who lived in a cottage close by but was *in* the house all the time – who could spear you with one glance.

But instead of a blistering stare, Carmelita looked up from the frying pan with a huge smile playing around her lips that she was trying – unsuccessfully – to suppress. "Good morning, Jennifer. Stetson went outside to do some chores; he will be back soon," she said, deftly flipping the bacon over without splattering grease like Jennifer always did, and then she slipped the grease splatter shield back in place over the cast-iron pan. "Did you sleep well?"

If Carmelita had white hair and a white beard – okay, and was male – she'd totally look like Santa Clause in that moment. Her eyes were twinkling with delight, and she seemed entirely too pleased with last night's activities.

Jennifer opened her mouth to demand how it was that Carmelita knew she'd spent the night in Stetson's bed, and then thought better of it. Some things were better left unknown.

"Uhhh…yes," she finally said, realizing she hadn't yet answered Carmelita's question. Jennifer stole another look at the grandmotherly woman, trying to decide if she was genuinely asking if she'd slept well, or if she wanted an actual report on what it was like to sleep with Stetson.

She wasn't sure if she could share deets like that with Carmelita. It just seemed wrong on so many levels.

But Carma just nodded her head, accepting Jennifer's terse answer, and set about serving up breakfast, which was, as usual, enough food to feed two Stetsons, and at least five Jennifers.

Jennifer promised herself that she'd do extra cardio down at the gym when she got back to Boise. But until then, do as the Romans do, right?

She dug into her waffles with gusto, chugging a bit of Carma's delicious coffee between bites. Something about sleeping with Stetson last night had completely rocked her world, and she didn't feel like she was on an even keel this morning. She was off-balance; prone to freaking out over absolutely nothing at all.

Coffee could only help this morning. Having a panic attack when still trying to wake up was not the premier start to her morning that she'd been hoping for.

"Stetson says he is going to take you on a tour of the farm today," Carmelita said as she began rinsing dishes and loading the dishwasher.

"Yeah, he offered the other day but…well, I didn't exactly come equipped with the right clothing for a ride on a four-wheeler, so we went shopping at Frank's yesterday to buy me some country clothing."

"Country clothing for a city girl, eh?" Carma said with a grin over her shoulder at Jennifer. "You better watch out. We will make you into a cowgirl yet."

"As long as I don't have to like country music, I can live with that," Jennifer said with a laugh. "I may be an Idaho girl, but I'm starting to realize that there's a world of difference between Boise and Sawyer. It's hard to believe that we're in the same country, let alone the same state."

"Oh, you have only just begun to see," Carmelita said with a teasing laugh. "Just wait until you realize how big this farm is. City people with their city lots — an acre seems large to them. There is nothing like a farm spread in a city."

Jennifer nodded politely, taking another bite of her food rather than saying anything in response to that comment. It was a ridiculous thing for Carmelita to say, of course — Jennifer knew *exactly* how big the farm was. The acreage was on the operating loan. If need be, she could state how many acres were being used for pasture versus how many were being planted in row crops. She knew how many cows Stetson had, and how many water shares the farm came with.

But still, it wasn't polite to rattle off numbers and show off, especially not to someone her senior, so she kept those facts to herself.

And, as she reminded herself, maybe she'd find something on this tour that wasn't on the paperwork; that could be sold to make the balloon payment.

It was only right that as the accountant on the case, she stay focused on what really mattered — saving the Miller Family Farm. Kissing and sex and licking nipples like strawberry ice cream could come later.

Right now, she had a job to do.

CHAPTER 36

STETSON

*H*E CHECKED his watch again. It was 8:33, two minutes after he'd last checked his watch. Was it too early to expect Jennifer to be up? It was a Saturday, plus he had kept her up half the night.

Yeah, it was much too early.

He stared at the haystack in front of him, trying to focus. He needed to calculate how much of his second-cutting hay was left. Then he'd know if he needed to buy some hay to supplement his own supply before winter hit.

He started walking as he thought, and before he realized it, he was climbing the front porch steps of the farmhouse and not at all counting hay bales like he was supposed to be.

Whoops.

Well, he could force himself to go back to the haystack and start counting – this time for real – but even as he thought it, his hand reached out to open up the front door. After all, there was no point in going all the way back without first at least checking to see if Jennifer was awake. Then after he verified that she was still in bed, he could go back to work.

He thought about the joyful grin that Carmelita had given him this morning, eyes sparkling as she'd asked him – bluntly – if he'd slept well last night. She looked like she'd just been given the present of a lifetime. He'd wanted to ask her how she knew, and then had stopped himself. There were some things that were better left unknown.

Not to mention that discussing his sex life with Carmelita just gave him the heebie-jeebies. One time, in high school, she'd asked him if he had rubbers while staring at the far wall over his shoulder, and it'd taken him a minute to realize that she was asking about condoms.

That conversation officially went down on record as the most awkward conversation ever held between the two of them, and he could only hope something like it was never repeated again.

"...after that, I told her that she could cook her own meals," Carmelita said as he walked into the kitchen.

"Who could cook their own meals?" Stetson asked, grabbing his coffee mug from breakfast that morning and refilling it. He leaned casually against the counter, trying to study Jennifer without being overly obvious about it, and failing miserably. Her hair was mussed, she still had no bra on, and his t-shirt and shorts still never looked better than they did in that moment.

But this morning's disheveled look came courtesy of him, and he felt his dick springing to attention with pride over that fact.

Down, boy, down. Springing a boner in front of Carmelita is not a good idea.

"That Michelle woman."

Stetson tore his eyes away from Jennifer's legs and the memory of them wrapped around him last night long enough to look at his housekeeper. "My ex? When did you tell her to make her own meals?" Inwardly, he couldn't help chuckling a little at the phrase "that Michelle woman." He'd dated her for six months and was engaged to her another two years after that, but Michelle and Carmelita had gotten along like oil and water. Carmelita had threatened to wear all black to the wedding, although in the end, she'd shown up in a black-and-white dress instead.

He figured that was quite the restraint, considering. And not a single I-told-you-so when Michelle hadn't bothered to show up at all.

That had required even more restraint.

"When she told me not to include so many carbohydrates in my dinners. She wanted me to cook a meal without a potato in it." Carmelita sniffed her indignation. "I told her that we live in Idaho, but she did not think that this mattered. *Güera.*"

Stetson tried to repress the grin he felt threatening

to erupt across his face, but he was totally losing that battle. *Güera*...he'd asked Carmelita a long time ago what that meant. She'd told him it meant someone who didn't understand anything outside of her own little view on the world.

If anyone deserved the nickname of *güera*, it was definitely Michelle.

Turning to Stetson, Jennifer shook her head mock seriously. "You were engaged to a woman who did not understand the sanctity of the potato? Some days, I'm not even sure who you are."

He shook his head, trying to glare at her for egging Carma on, but mostly just laughing. "Are you ready to go?" he asked, trying to ignore that comment. His eyes swept down her legs and back up again. "You appear ready for a pajama party, not a tour of a farm," he added dryly.

"I'll hurry!" she promised, jumping out of her chair. "We got sidetracked, swapping war stories. Sometime, you'll have to tell me what you saw in this Michelle."

Stetson opened his mouth to ask his housekeeper *exactly* which tales she'd shared when someone pounded on the front door, loud and angry. Everyone froze, staring at each other. Just moments later, the knocking came again, even louder this time.

"I think you should answer it before they knock the door down," Carmelita said, worry drawing her eyebrows together. "Maybe someone is hurt. Your brothers?"

Stetson hurried to the front door, his boots echoing on the oak floors as he practically ran through the house. What if Declan had gotten in a car wreck? Hit a deer? Was dead, just like their mother?

He yanked the door open, heart pounding, only to find a shorter, balding man standing on the porch, his hand raised in the air, ready to knock a third time. Stetson jerked his head back, staring down at the man. He didn't recognize him, and the man didn't have an official uniform on, which likely meant he wasn't an EMT or cop, come to give him bad news.

So why the hell was he here?

Just as he was opening his mouth to ask that, the man puffed up his chest and announced regally, "I am here for Jennifer Kendall."

"Paul?" came Jennifer's voice from behind Stetson.

CHAPTER 37

JENNIFER

JENNIFER SLIPPED underneath Stetson's arm, propped up in the corner of the doorway, to stand on the front porch and glare at her ex-fiancé. "What are you doing here?" she demanded.

Paul's eyes followed her form up and down, making her feel like she'd just taken a bath in used motor oil, before he finally spat out, "Is this how you dress at a client's house?"

"This is how I dress on a Saturday morning. I repeat – what are you doing here?"

"Well, after I called *and* texted you – multiple times, I might add – and you didn't answer, other than those few rude texts that I just couldn't believe were coming from you, I decided to come up here and talk to you in person. I guess your overgrown ape here is the one who'd been sending those awful texts to me? Cell phone conversations are private, you know," he said, glaring up over Jennifer's shoulder. "You shouldn't be reading her texts, let alone replying on her behalf—"

"As happy as it makes me that you understand and believe in a woman's right to talk to whomever she pleases," Jennifer cut in, trying to keep the sarcasm from dripping *too* much off her tongue, "you should know that Stetson has never so much as touched my phone. Unlike other people, he doesn't think that I'm going to cheat on him every time he leaves the room."

Okay, so it was possible that she'd given up completely on the idea of keeping sarcasm out of her voice. Paul's eyes bugged out. "I did not think you'd cheat on me *every* time I left the room!" he huffed. "Hyperbole does not suit you."

"And hypocrisy doesn't suit you," Jennifer said blandly. "They always say that whatever you're worried about in a partner is what you're actually doing yourself. Hmmm…is that why you spent three years thinking that I was cheating on you, and always making me re-confirm to you again and again that I hadn't? How many women, exactly, did you give *mouth-to-mouth lessons* to while we were engaged?"

"Well, I never—" Paul sputtered, his face growing red with rage. "I am here," he drew himself up imperiously, bringing his height to the full 3/4's of an inch that he had on her, "to tell you that if you promise to behave yourself, I am willing to take you back."

Jennifer could practically feel the anger pulsating

off Stetson in waves, but she didn't dare retreat back into him. She was going to stand up for herself this time, dammit. She'd spent a whole year working through self-help books after she'd left this snake, trying to figure out why she'd put up with Paul, time after awful time when he'd denigrated her. Told her she was less than. And then the final insult – to find him in bed with a coworker, Lizzie, who had *much* larger boobs than Jennifer could ever hope to have, even if she paid for breast implants or something else equally as ridiculous.

But instead of laying into him when she'd found them together in bed, she'd run away, crying. She'd gotten her stuff out of his apartment while he was at work. She'd quit the hospital and had never gone back. The Old Jennifer hadn't wanted to talk to him, ever again.

After a year of self-help books and digging in deep, though, she'd made a lot of realizations about herself, and New Jennifer had a backbone that made her willing to share those thoughts instead of just forcing herself to bury them deep inside.

Well, now was her chance to say all of the things that Old Jennifer wouldn't say to him, and she was starting to realize that it felt good.

Damn good.

"That's funny," she drawled in her best thick Idaho accent, "'cause I don't recall *wanting* to come back."

"Now, Pumpkin," he said, instantly changing

tactics. He was as transparent as plastic wrap, and about as personable. What had she seen in him all those years ago? As her eyes flicked up and down his body, she realized she had a hard time remembering now. "You don't know what you're saying. It must've been quite the shock to see me show up here, but that doesn't mean you should be hast—"

"How many nurses?" she asked bluntly.

"What?" Paul was staring at her. Stetson was shifting from foot to foot behind her, probably just waiting for the signal to pound the guy into the ground.

Jennifer ignored it all. She was in control here.

"How many nurses have you slept with since I left you?"

"I don't know what that has to do wi—"

"Because I heard one time from another nurse back at the hospital that you tend to cycle through relationships every six months or so. I was the only one dumb enough to last as long as I did. So I'm just wanting to do the math. Did you find any other doormats to trample all over for years? Or did they all get out at the six-month mark?"

"This is what I've been trying to tell you!" he exclaimed triumphantly. "I know that you're jealous of the other women in my life, but I have to be able to work with females, Pumpkin. You can't keep throwing these little temper tantrums."

"Huh. So faster than six months, eh? What did they average – three months? Four months? Did a nurse figure out what an ass you are and drop you at two months?"

The flush that spread across Paul's face was the only indication that he heard her.

"How'd you get here?" she asked, abruptly changing subjects. He jerked, startled by the switch.

"I dr-drove," he sputtered. "Of course. I'm not going to walk all the way from Boi—"

"How did you *know* to come here?" she asked, interrupting him again. She'd been raised to never interrupt others, but damn if she wasn't finding a perverse pleasure in doing it to Paul.

Finally, all of the things she'd wanted to say and do, but had never thought she'd have the chance. *This* was her chance. Her legs felt shaky and her head felt like it was floating off her shoulders from the adrenaline rush pumping through her veins. Standing up to Paul was scary and thrilling and amazing and horrible, all at once.

Some part of her knew that Stetson was behind her 100%, both figuratively and literally, and would be willing to take a swing at the guy if need be. She also knew that Carmelita was hovering back there too, no doubt waiting for her chance to jump into the conversation and tell Paul to go eat McDonald's food – the worst insult *ever* – but this was Jennifer's show. She was running it. She was standing up for herself.

Even if it made her want to throw up a little bit, it was *totally* worth it.

"I asked down at the bank," Paul sniffed in his

best "duh" voice. "Yesterday afternoon. Then I had to put together a suitcase and an itinerary for our date that we'd have together once I picked you up. So I couldn't actually leave until this morning."

A small part of her – okay, a giant-ass part of her – was dying to know what was on this itinerary, but she didn't want to get sidetracked. She had facts to gather, dammit.

Stetson started to speak, his anger at high tide at this point, but Jennifer held up her hand, not even looking back over her shoulder.

This was her fight. She would take the worm down.

"Intermountain West Bank & Loan told you where I was," she repeated softly, staring at Paul, her eyes boring into his.

"Well yes, of course," he huffed. "I told your boss, Gregory, that it was of the utmost importance that I speak to you. Once he found out that I was a doctor, why, he gave me the information right away, as he should have." He nodded once, as if agreeing with himself.

Of *course* he agreed with himself.

"Good to know. I wanted to make sure I implicated the right employee on Monday when I filed a complaint with the bank headquarters over this. I'll be sure to state that you are my source of this information. I have your phone number, so the bank president can call you for more details if he'd like."

He sputtered for a moment, his eyes growing wide

as he looked at her, and finally, he spat out, "You've changed! You're *nothing* like my old Jennifer." It was the worst insult he could think of to dish out.

She sent him a huge smile. "I know!" she said with a laugh. "Isn't it wonderful? When I think back to the Old Jennifer – the one willing to put up with all that I did – it makes my skin crawl. Every change that I've made in the last two years has been because I realized that I didn't like you, but even more importantly, I didn't like *me* when I was with you. Now, if you'll excuse us, Stetson and I were about to go out on a tour of his farm, and you're not welcome to join us."

"So the overgrown ape *is* your boyfriend, eh?" he sneered. "Just wait until your boss hears that you're dating a client!"

"Well now," Stetson rumbled in his deep voice, his patience completely gone, "I suggest you walk back to your car, get in it, and drive on back to Boise. Right now. If you insist on making me escort you off my property, you're not gonna like how I do it."

"You wouldn't dare touch me!" Paul said indignantly. "I am a *doctor*! No court in the land would side with a redneck over me."

Stetson chuckled. "The sheriff of Long Valley hunts on my land every fall. We're coming up on hunting season. Do you really think that he'd take the side of some city slicker who he's never met, over his hunting buddy and his chance to hunt in the best elk territory in the county?"

So that's *why he decorates with elk horns…*

She forced her mind back to the topic at hand.

"I'll…I'll call him right now!" Paul threatened, pulling his cell phone out of his pocket.

"You go right on ahead," Stetson said blandly. "And while you're at it, remind him to put in for the elk tag draw for this fall. I'd hate to have him miss another elk season because he forgot to fill out some paperwork. He was damn busy last year, and I had to make do with hunting with the deputy sheriff instead."

Paul's eyes darted between Jennifer and Stetson, clearly trying to decide if Stetson was being serious. His fingers hovered over his phone, undecided.

So, Stetson being the kind soul that he was, helped him along in the decision-making process. Picking Jennifer up and setting her gently to the side, he was on the porch in just seconds. He grabbed the collar of Paul's shirt and the waistband of his pants in one smooth motion, and then Paul was flying off the front porch, through the air, to land in the same puddle she'd stepped in the second morning she'd come out to the farm. It was smaller now, since the rain had stopped yesterday morning, but it still wasn't *small* by any stretch of the imagination.

Paul rolled over, looking down at his ruined clothes and back up at Stetson. "You…you…" he spluttered, as Stetson leaned against one of the porch columns, looking on as if watching a fascinating play that was being put on in his front yard.

Jennifer moved up next to him and slipped her

arm around his waist. "Hi, darlin'," she said casually, and then grinned up at him. "Nice arm."

"Thanks!" he said, grinning back. "My brothers used to do that move all the time on me. I guess it's just fun to finally be able to pull it on someone else."

They turned to watch Paul scramble to his feet, blustering like a bedraggled rooster about how he was going to call his lawyer as soon as he got back to civilization.

"You do that," Stetson drawled. "And be sure to tell your lawyer that you gained my address illegally, and that you were asked to leave in a polite way before I helped you along. I'm sure your lawyer will want to hear *all* of the details."

Face red, Paul slid into his Ferrari and tore off, wheels throwing up chunks of mud and gravel. They watched him go, Jennifer waving gaily as he did, her stomach practically floating with happiness. With the help of Stetson, she'd actually faced down and defeated a man who'd held way too much power over her for way too long. What a feeling it was.

"Ouch!" Stetson yelped, pulling away from Jennifer and rubbing the back of his head as he turned to glare down at Carmelita. Jennifer jerked too, completely startled. She'd been lost in her own little world. Had Carmelita just smacked Stetson on the back of the head?

Before she could ask what just happened, Carma smiled up at Stetson, a huge, jaw-cracking grin. "You did good, *mi hijo*. Your parents," she crossed her ample chest, "are smiling down on you. Now! I must go wash bedding. It is time for me to do *my* job." She hurried back into the house, dabbing at the corners of her eyes with her apron as she went.

As quickly as the surge of power and pride had filled Jennifer's soul, they went rushing back out again, leaving the stench of shame in its wake. She was so embarrassed. How had this happened?

"I'm so sorry!" she gasped. "Oh God. It's so unprofessional to have my ex show up here like this. You...*argh!*"

Tripping over her own tongue. It was a thing.

What she'd stopped herself from actually saying out loud was that it was *way* too early in their relationship – if you could call one night of heavenly sex to even be a relationship – to deal with this kind of drama. So. Not. Cool. He probably thought this happened every weekend.

Dammit!

This was the sort of thing that you confessed to your new boyfriend after a year of dating and two bottles of wine.

Not like *this*.

"Sometime, you'll have to tell me what you saw in this Paul," he said, looking down at her with a huge grin on his face. It took her brain a few seconds to realize that he was mimicking her comment that she'd made, *right* before Paul showed up.

She buried her face in her hands, feeling her face turn a pulsating red from the sly repartee. "Truce," she mumbled. "Truce!" she said again, pulling her hands away and looking up, up, up into Stetson's face. "I won't make fun of Michelle if you don't make fun of Paul."

"Damn," Stetson said, pulling her up against him to bury his face in her hair and draw in a deep breath. "But I had so many things to make fun of about my choice to date Michelle for so long. Why, we'd just barely gotten started!"

Jennifer laughed against his chest. "It does seem to defy logic, doesn't it?" she asked rhetorically. "I never saw Paul again after I found him and Lizzie in bed together. I made damn sure of it. I'd often wondered – some small part of me – what it'd be like if I did see him again. I never thought I'd be astounded by the question, 'What on earth did I see in you?' I always thought I'd struggle with standing up to him or feeling hurt all over again by his betrayal. But astonishment? Yeah, totally didn't guess that." She shrugged, keeping her face firmly buried against Stetson. It was less embarrassing that way. "I also never thought I'd be able to stand up to him like I did. It was the best feeling in the world, honestly! No wonder guys like to get into fights and just duke things out."

"You thought that was a fight?" Stetson asked. She could feel his chest vibrate with silent laughter against her cheek. "The next time Wyatt and I have a 'discussion,' remind me to invite you to watch. What just happened with Paul is practically a tea party in comparison."

"I don't like fighting. Or arguing," she said, still firmly nestled against him. She wasn't quite ready to pull away and meet his gaze yet. "Why do you think I worked so hard to avoid Paul after I found him cheating on me? I just wanted to walk away and pretend it never happened. It's not healthy."

"Hey, I've been tempted to avoid confrontation," Stetson said, nestling her further against his body and swaying lightly as they talked. "The other day, when I saw Declan and Wyatt's trucks were here, all I wanted to do was turn around and run back to town. I knew it wasn't going to go well. Any time Wyatt and I breathe the same air, it doesn't go well."

"Yeah, but you didn't actually run away," she pointed out logically. "I always have. Before today, that is. And the only reason I didn't today is because I couldn't. I don't have a car to drive away in, and I don't have a house to hide in. I was stuck."

"And the only reason I didn't run away the other day is because I knew it would only make things worse between Wyatt and I. Harvest is coming. I can't stop the change of the seasons. So I was forced to go in and talk to him, despite me wanting to do almost anything else but."

He was running his fingers through her hair methodically, scalp to ends, as they swayed in the warm summer air. "Don't be so tough on yourself," he said, just above a whisper. "You have a lot more backbone than you give yourself credit for. Despite my lecture on which meals you can eat and what

Carmelita can make for you, you didn't drive back to Boise and tell your boss that he can foreclose on the property, even though I know now that's what he wanted to hear. Why didn't you?"

"Recommend foreclosure right off the bat and just walk away, you mean?"

"Yeah. Knowing what I know now…on one side, you had a jackass of a farmer who made you feel like shit for being here, and on the other side, you had a boss who was pushing you to just recommend foreclosure. In your shoes, I think it would be hard to still do your job, especially since you had no real incentive to do so."

"Well, because it is my job." She shrugged a little. Her eyes were closed and she was just enjoying the heartbeat of Stetson, steady and strong. "If I quit every time someone was rude to me, I would never do my job. I can't say you exactly made me feel welcome, but I've had other irate clients before. In fact, they usually start out that way; it's rare if they don't. I've learned to just shrug it off for the most part. Sometimes, if I'm lucky, I can change their mind. Sometimes, especially when I can't find a way for the business to be saved, I can't change their mind. That's when my parentage gets called into question."

He was silent for a moment, and then he began laughing. "No wonder Carmelita likes you," he said around his laughter. "That was the classiest way I've ever heard of someone being referred to as a bastard."

"Well, that and Carmelita just has good taste," she told him. "Obviously."

"Obviously," Stetson repeated, still laughing. "So, are we gonna go upstairs and canoodle some more, or are we gonna go on a tour of the farm?"

"Canoodle?!" She let out a snort of laughter. "It is 2016, right? We didn't jump back to 1816 without me knowing it?"

"If you grew up with Carmelita standing over you, willing to whack you on the back of the head for the most inconsequential swear word, you quickly find substitutes to use. That tendency spreads to other... delicate topics of discussion."

It was her turn to have her shoulders shake with laughter. "Fair enough," she allowed. That laughter quickly turned to quiet moans of lust when Stetson drew his hands up her sides and across to her chest, across her hardened nipples.

"If I remember right, I have some strawberry ice cream to lick," he said softly in her ear.

It was the damnedest thing, to feel lust and shame battle each other inside of her. Lust, because what he was doing felt so damn good. But shame, because she'd spent years being told she wasn't enough. The old fears and doubts were still there; one night of him saying nice things couldn't erase years of programming and negativity.

She froze in his arms, still as a statue as she tried to reason through everything flashing through her mind.

"What? What's wrong?" Stetson asked, pulling back so he could look her in the face.

"I just realized something," she breathed, forcing herself to look up and into his bottomless brown eyes. She needed to stop hiding, even if it was just her hiding her face against his chest.

Stetson stood there, his arms lightly encircling her, waiting ever-so-patiently for her to speak. A light summer breeze had her hair dancing in it, but Stetson pushed it back for her, letting her gather her thoughts.

"When I left Paul, I spent a long time reading self-help books and books on domestic abuse. He may never have hit me, but he hurt me in ways that can't be seen. He made me start to doubt my sanity, by questioning if I'd been flirting with an orderly or security guard at work. I hadn't been, but after a while…it's amazing how it can start to screw with your mind. Maybe I had been staring at the security guard without realizing it. Maybe I had laughed flirtatiously when a guy told me a joke, and I just hadn't realized it. Maybe Paul was right, and I was just slowly going nuts – not in control of my own body.

"But after I left him, I started to realize that this was what the psychologists call 'gas lighting,' where a person makes you start to question your own reality. I worked through all of that, and finally came to the realization that Paul is just sick upstairs."

She bit her lip as she looked up into his deep brown eyes, worrying it before forcing her to finally say her realization. "But through it all, I never dealt with the emotional abuse of him making me feel ugly. It's funny because somehow, I was both beautiful enough to tempt men to flirt with me, even though everyone knew I was engaged to Paul, *and* ugly enough that Paul sometimes had to force himself to sleep with me, because he knew that I crave physical intimacy. But he'd tell me beforehand what a sacrifice he was making, for me. How kind he was being, to me. He even told me one time that my natural odor was a turn-off, so I started wearing heavy perfume, trying to cover me up.

"I dealt with some of this stuff, but after all this time, I'm realizing – I haven't dealt with it all. I'm still kind of broken inside, Stetson. Last night was a lot of fun, but we'd both been drinking and…you don't have to still pretend to want me if you don't anymore. This…this is who I am. This is the real me. I have issues; I'm not gonna lie. You might not want to deal with all of this baggage, and I…"

She stopped, and then whispered, "I wouldn't blame you if you wanted to walk away."

The light breeze carried her words off, floating on the current, swirling over the farm and away into the world, dissipating, dissolving into nothing at all.

Maybe they could just forget everything. Maybe she could go back to the office and add up numbers and force logic into the world, one Excel column at a time, and he could go back to wrestling calves and driving tractor and they could pretend that nothing had happened. *"What, that banker? Yeah, she came and looked over the books for a while, but she's gone back to Boise now."*

He lifted her chin gently but inexorably, forcing her to look him in the eye. "Baby, I have a glued-together left eyebrow, an eye turning beautiful colors, and a hand bandaged up from accidentally punching the front of my grandfather's tractor. I have so much baggage, I'm gonna start ordering matching sets, complete with little wheels on the bottom so I can more easily tow them along behind me. How do you think I got such rock-hard muscles?" He flexed and pointed to his sizable bicep. "That's from carrying my baggage everywhere I've gone since I was a small child."

He scooped her up into his arms effortlessly, carrying her back inside the house, pushing the front door closed behind him with the heel of his boot. "Sometime, I ought to tell you how I spent years thinking that I killed my mother. Hey Carmelita," he shouted, looking up from Jennifer's gaping mouth, "Jennifer and I are gonna go study some spreadsheets. In detail. No need to come help us figure things out – I think we've got this one."

"Spreadsheets…your mother…" Jennifer sputtered as Stetson took the stairs two at a time, carrying her in his arms like she weighed no more than a newborn babe. "You're gonna hurt your back, carrying me around like this," she informed him, trying to glare seriously up at him.

"Well then, it'll be worth every twinge of pain I suffer," he said, closing the door to the master bedroom behind him. "And anyway, you're as light as a feather. I could carry you around all day long." He dropped her on the bed and then crawled in after her. "But right now, I have other things on my mind…"

CHAPTER 38

STETSON

*D*ROPPING JENNIFER onto the bed and watching *all* the right parts of her bounce was definitely the highlight of his day.

Well, throwing Paul into that puddle was a close second. But that was more satisfying, whereas watching Jennifer smile up at him, visibly pushing the doubt away and choosing to focus on the here and now…that was just damn sexy.

He quickly skimmed her (his?) shorts off her hips, and the ratty t-shirt off her body, leaving – just as he'd expected – a completely naked Jennifer underneath. "You always come down to breakfast only half clothed?" he growled, nibbling his way up the sexiest pair of legs he ever did see. There was this cord of muscle that ran up the back side of her calf that he wanted to follow wherever it led. Preferably up north, but he'd follow it almost anywhere at this point.

"When you're as small as I am up top," she said

with a shrug and a hitch in her voice as he began sucking on the calf muscle, "bras are more of a fashion statement, rather than a necessi-ty." Her voice broke on the last word as she groaned with lust. "Oh, oh, oh, that feels…"

And then she was tossing her head back and forth on the bed, moaning and mumbling to herself. He permitted himself a self-satisfied smirk. Seeing what his lips did to her *definitely* did something to him.

"I'll have to remember this for future reference," he murmured as he worked his way up her thighs. The calf muscle had disappeared, but her thighs were even more enticing, if that was even possible, and he hadn't even gotten to the grand finale yet.

He nosed her swatch of curls, breathing in the unique scent that was pure Jennifer Kendall, and sighing with pure lust. He'd never met a woman who smelled so amazing.

Which reminded him…

"Babe?"

"Ye…yeah?" she finally got out, legs spasming with pleasure.

"Paul is an idiot. And he needs to have his nose fixed."

And with that, he finally gave her what she wanted as he licked his way up her delicious pink pussy.

Pink pussy, pink tits…

"My favorite color is pink," he announced as he blew cold air over her clit.

"Ohhhhhh…" Jennifer exclaimed, but somehow, he wasn't thinking that it was in excitement over his color preferences. The arch of her back, her clasping at the bedspread…

She might like pink, but probably not *that* much.

He smiled with self-satisfaction again. Teaching Jennifer how much fun it was in bed?

Priceless.

CHAPTER 39

JENNIFER

*J*ENN WOKE UP with a mumbled sigh. Something amazing had happened, or maybe that was just a dream she'd had, but her thighs were sticky with cum and so just a dream didn't seem right but—

And then she felt hard muscle, lying next to her. Her eyes popped open and she stared at her bedmate. She was in Stetson's bed – *again* – but this time she was waking up next to him instead of him being gone and then she remembered, remembered everything she'd told him on the front porch – why the hell had she told him all of that?! – and she wasn't breathing right and then his eyes fluttered open and he grinned lazily, a grin that quickly transformed into panic.

"What's wrong?" he asked, reaching out for her and pulling her against him. "Did you have a bad dream?"

"I just…why did I say…why did I tell you all of…"

She breathed in through her nose and out through her mouth, trying to calm her racing heart.

"Why did you tell me all of that stuff while we were out on the front porch together?" he asked softly.

She had her eyes squeezed tightly shut as she nodded. *Idiot, idiot, idiot. Now he can* really *hurt you.*

"Maybe because you know I'd never use something like that against you."

Her eyes popped open, swimming with tears and disbelief as she stared at him. But she *didn't* know that. He could!

"I don't trust easily," he said softly. "I actually had that thought just the other day. About you. That I had to be careful about what I told you and how much I let you in. I think that honestly, though, I've already let you in more than any other woman I've ever dated, including Michelle. It's not easy to bare your soul to someone else. All I can do is give you my word not to abuse that trust."

She bit on her lower lip, contemplating what he said. Could she trust him? The last time she'd believed that a male had good intentions, she'd ended up in an emotionally abusive relationship for years.

But mostly, she just felt overwhelmed. Wrung out. Waking up twice in one day in a panic, yelling at Paul, finally telling him everything she'd wanted to tell him but never had, opening her wounds up to Stetson's gaze…

It was exhausting.

As if he knew what she was thinking, he pushed her hair out of her face and said softly, "I think we've had enough serious, life-altering discussions for one day, don't you? I think it's about time we have that farm tour I've been promising you for two days straight."

She nodded, pushing her worries to the back of her mind. He was right – she really didn't have much choice except to trust him. It was too late to take her words back now. She could freak out later, after the farm tour was over; maybe tonight, as she laid in bed – by herself – and tried to process everything.

No sleeping with Stetson again until you've thought through all of this. By yourself.

She would be a good girl…later. For now, she wanted a break from it all.

"Deal," she said, and swung her legs off his four-poster bed. After hurrying into the guest bathroom to clean up and get ready for the tour, she peeked back into the master bedroom and found it empty. She headed downstairs instead, where she found Stetson and Carmelita talking in hushed tones.

Carmelita looked up with a warm smile on her face. "Stetson says he is finally going to show you the Miller Farm. You two go have fun. It is important to relax after such a man dares to come here and says what he did." She made shooing motions, pushing them through the door. "Go, go. I will make a pie. You can have dessert when you come back."

She closed the door behind them.

Jennifer looked up at Stetson and laughed. "Is she always this bossy?" she asked dryly.

"You have no idea," he muttered, grabbing her hand and pulling it through the crook of his elbow. "I think Carmelita was a mother hen in a past life."

They wandered down a large, sloping hill that ended in an even larger clearing ringed with forest. "I keep the four-wheeler in here," he said, pulling her towards a small shed off to the side. "We can ride double."

After he pulled the machine out and had her securely in place, scooted up tight against his broad back, her arms wrapped around him, he took off slowly, skirting around the base of the hill and towards a cluster of buildings.

"I'll take you to Nudges' arena first," he said over his shoulder, turning between a large red barn and a smaller, faded wooden outbuilding. "Every girl loves cute cows."

She tried to keep her skepticism to herself. She'd seen her fair share of cows as she drove past fields in the Treasure Valley – once you got out of Boise proper, there was a fair amount of farmland between sprawling housing developments – and had never thought of them as being particularly cute. Healthy, content, at ease...sure. But "cute" seemed like it was taking it a step too far.

He pulled up to a corral and helped her off the four-wheeler. She looked up and spotted a pink nose sticking through the weathered, gray slats of the corral. Stetson guided her over to a gate and shut it securely behind them. "So, this is Nudges. You might have already guessed why we call him that."

The sturdy little guy was busy shoving his nose up against her arm so hard, it was lifting her arm up in the air. "Hi!" she said with a startled laugh, and began scratching him behind his ears. He closed his eyes with apparent satisfaction, his incredibly long lashes laying against his cheeks in bliss.

"Are all cows' eyelashes this long?" she asked as she started to scratch harder. Nudges was getting so into it, he was probably going to fall over any minute now.

"Yup. Keeps the flies out of them. You'll never find longer eyelashes than are on cows and horses."

Jennifer pulled her hand away and Nudges followed it with his tongue, giving her a thick swipe up the hand. She laughed with delight.

"How old is he?" she asked. "And where's his momma?"

"Funny story, that," Stetson said, grimacing. "I paid a stud fee to bring in a bull from southern Utah this past year, and after he hung out for a month, having done his duty, the owner was driving here to pick him up and take him back home, when he gets in this massive car wreck. He spent a month in the hospital – internal injuries and the whole bit. So of course, I'm hanging onto the bull in the meanwhile, and where was he hanging out? With the girls. I don't have corral fencing strong enough to keep a horny bull in. If I have to keep a bull here, it's gonna be in with my girls. If he's gettin' some on the regular, well then, he'll be easy as pie to be around and won't be doing his best to knock my fences down."

"Some things in the animal world remind me so much of the men I know…" Jennifer said with a laugh and roll of her eyes.

"I'd never try to deny it," Stetson said with a naughty grin. Nudges had wandered over to him as they were talking, apparently ready to get his second dose of loving from the humans in his corral, and so Stetson stroked Nudges' side as he talked. Nudges really got into it; leaning up against Stetson's legs with almost his entire body weight plastered against him.

Stetson didn't even seem to notice.

Jennifer was pretty sure that if Nudges did that to her, they'd be in a pile on the ground together. Nudges weighed more than she did, she was almost sure of it.

"So anyway, apparently one of the girls hadn't caught before – one of the younger heifers – but after the bull's extended stay…well, she's no longer a heifer. Let's just put it that way." He grinned at her lasciviously. "The bad news is, in cow years, she'd *just* hit puberty, and just like you don't particularly want a 16-year-old girl pregnant, you don't want young heifers pregnant either. They have no idea how to be a mom, and since everyone else was way ahead of her in the pregnancy cycle, none of the moms who'd been around the block a time or two would show her what to do. By the time she gave birth, she was in a high stress mental state, and she immediately rejected Nudges. Wouldn't have a damn thing to do with him. High stress will do that to a cow, especially a young one."

"Wow." Jennifer just stared at him. "Wow. Like, that should be a soap opera storyline or something. I had no idea…"

"Cows have amazingly complex social structures in place," Stetson said with a shrug. "I've been working with them for about a decade now, and I don't even pretend to understand them fully. A lot like the females I know."

Jennifer rolled her eyes, ignoring that comment. For now. "So how is Nudges still here, if his mom wouldn't nurse him? Did you bottle feed him?"

"Oh *hell* no," Stetson said, laughing. "I just don't have the time. You know who's really good at bottle feeding? Christian's sister, Yesenia."

"Your foreman's sister?"

Stetson nodded. "She's 16 and wanted Nudges as her 4-H project. I knew there was no way I could take care of him, so I gladly turned him over to her. As you can tell, he's just about the friendliest boy you'll ever meet." He was still stroking Nudges down the side as he continued, "She's done a bang-up job with him. Bottle fed him for the first month, then switched him to hot feed. Honestly, she's not going to win with him. He's too far behind the rest of the steers that'll be shown in the 4-H fair because of being born later, but all in all, he's been catching up. He'll be a good showing for her, and she'll make a nice bit of cash from the sale that she can save for college."

"Sale…" Jennifer looked down at the adorable boy who'd made his way over to the feed bucket, slurping down dinner. The idea of selling him off so he could go to a slaughterhouse…

Stetson put his hand under her chin. "I know it's hard, especially when they have personality like Nudges does. But it's how I make my living. A T-bone steak comes from somewhere. I supply that somewhere. I can't afford to be squeamish about it."

She nodded, looking down at the ground as she did so. He was right, of course. But he was also right about it being hard.

Rows and columns in a spreadsheet were so much more containable. So much more manageable. So much less painful.

"Ready to take a look around the barn?" he asked.

"Sure," she said, trying to put a brave face on it. She was fine. She was totally fine. She followed him out of the corral, waiting for him as he shut the gate behind them.

Totally fine.

CHAPTER 40

STETSON

*A*FTER A RESTLESS NIGHT in bed where Stetson had to take his trusty companion out on yet another less-than-satisfactory date, he got up bright and early. He tried to work a little less on Sundays, if only so he didn't get the death glare from Carmelita over it, but there were still chores that had to be done every day, no matter what.

After a quick shower, he headed outside to get water troughs filled and check on the wheat and corn. Everything was looking great, and for once, Stetson had a smile on his face that he just couldn't wipe away. More than the cows and the crops, his whole life was looking fine. Jennifer hadn't yet found that magic wand that would save the Miller Farm, but he had faith in her that she would. She was too damn smart not to. Or at least plead her way through to some sort of arrangement on his behalf. She'd know what to do better than he ever could. He just had to trust her.

There was that word again.

Trusting a woman who could hurt him…well, that was a tough row to hoe. He'd been telling Jennifer the truth the other night, about how women held more power in their little pinky than they even realized, but he doubted she truly believed him.

Whether or not it was actually true.

Yesenia pulled up in the family's little two-wheel-drive Toyota, here for her chores for the day. Stetson waved to her as she jumped out, a pair of beat-up jeans and an even older flannel shirt tied at the waist. "Hi Stetson!" she said with a smile, her long straight hair hanging down her back in a black cascade. At only 16, she was already starting to fill out. She was gonna be one gorgeous girl when she got older. "How is my Nudges doing?"

"Good," he said with a big smile. "I think he's putting on weight at a great clip. How's his feed look – do I need to order some more?" He'd meant to check that yesterday when he'd been showing Jennifer around, but had somehow gotten sidetracked. Possibly by the cutest ass he ever did see, but that was a given at this point.

"Nah. I think we have another week or so." They wandered into the corral together and she loved on Nudges, who was happily living up to his name, joyfully basking in the attention she was slathering on. "Thank you again for the feed," she said. "It means—"

"No problem," he said, waving it away. Yesenia

thanked him every time the topic came up, which was embarrassing as hell.

He hadn't mentioned this particular fact to Jennifer during their tour because…well, money. The topic was a touchy one. He didn't want to tell her that he was paying for all of the feed for a 4-H project for someone else, when he couldn't even make his payment on his loan. But honestly, a few hundred dollars wouldn't even make a dent in the interest on the loan, and it meant a lot more to Yesenia to be able to pay for this project. Times were tight for everyone; helping Yesenia make some extra money on the side was worth it.

"I will give you half the money at the sale, I promise," Yesenia continued. Stetson cocked an eyebrow at her.

"We've gone over this before. You're going to put *all* of it into a savings account to save for college. Speaking of, are you reading this summer like you're supposed to?" She was enrolled in the advanced English class at the high school, with a stupidly long list of books she was assigned to read before school started this fall. A guy could enjoy a western or a thriller every once in a while, but it seemed like to him, the teacher was taking this whole advanced English class to an unnecessary level.

"I just finished *Pride and Prejudice*," she announced proudly. "Mr. Darcy reminds me of you, actually."

Stetson was still trying to process the idea of voluntarily reading a Jane Austen book when

Yesenia's words registered. "What? Why?" he asked, startled.

Yesenia looked up from her pettings of Nudges and said, "Pride. You both have a lot of it."

Stetson just nodded, taken aback. What could he say to a 16-year-old's comment like that? "Right. Well, I better go check on the herd. Make sure no one's run off in the night. See ya around."

He tugged on the brim of his hat as Yesenia set about cleaning out Nudge's corral.

Mr. Darcy? Him? Wasn't that book set in England or France or something? He'd never even been outside of the intermountain states; he sure as hell hadn't travelled to another country.

Although Yesenia's English was excellent, he couldn't help but wonder if something had gotten lost in translation somewhere along the way.

CHAPTER 41

JENNIFER

*T*HREE DAYS. It had been three days of heaven in Stetson's arms.

Except, it was quickly turning to hell as she stared down at the ledger in front of her. The tour of the farm had revealed a couple of tractors that were needed to harvest Stetson's crops, cows that were already contracted to be sold to the restaurants in Boise, rolls of bailing twine and rusty bolts, an ancient tractor from the 1950s, fields of corn, hay, and wheat, and one adorable steer who was the property of Yesenia.

Well, and the tour revealed that as always, Carmelita was right. The farm *was* much larger than Jennifer had realized. Somehow, bland numbers on a page didn't mean nearly as much as seeing the wide open spaces for herself. The farm had gone on for forever, it seemed, nestled up against the Goldfork Mountains.

Stetson pointed to the mountains and said that they'd had their chunk of the mountainside checked for minerals or gems – Idaho *was* the Gem State, after all – but there hadn't been enough there to make it worthwhile to set up a whole mining operation. His dad had even looked at selling the pine trees that dotted the mountainside to a logging company, but the trees were too sparse and the terrain was too steep and rocky to make building a road up it worthwhile.

Worthwhile.

It was a word Jennifer was starting to hate.

It was the same word Stetson had used when she'd brought up the topic of splitting off a portion of the farm and selling it to an area farmer. They had been standing on the back porch when she'd suggested it, and Stetson had pulled her out into the sunshine as he talked her through it.

"If I tried to sell that chunk over there," he'd said, pointing into the sunshine, "we'd have to build a road through the rest of the property to give access to it, and then give a right-away to the new owner for that road. It'd cost me as much in time and materials and lost productivity since I can't graze a road, that I'd lose money doing it. Same with that piece over there," he'd said, swinging his arm to the right. Her gaze had followed his arm, happy to be staring into something that *wasn't* direct sunlight. "Except with that one, it's even worse because I would have to build a full-sized bridge over the canal that could support any kind of rig the new owner would want to drive down it. Do you have any idea what kind of price tag a bridge like that would have? It just isn't worthwhile.

"And my neighbor to the west," he'd said, jerking his thumb, "is looking for a buyer for his own property. If I could afford to, I'd be snatching that piece up from him. I could double my corn crop every year with that farmland to work with. But I can't afford to buy it, and he sure as hell doesn't want to buy from me. The last thing he wants is *more* land. He's older and looking to stop working so damn hard, and his boys don't want the farm. He says he's spent too many mornings in the seat of a tractor; he wants his ass in a cabana instead." He'd shot Jennifer a grin. "I tried to put that image outta my head as quick as it arrived. I suggest you do the same."

A wrinkly old farmer in board shorts, hanging out with a coconut drink in his hand.

Yeah, that was an image she'd be happy to never think about again.

So what *was* worthwhile? Jennifer scrubbed at her eyes with the palms of her hands. She didn't know, but she sure as hell better figure it out, and quick. Greg wasn't going to put up with her continuing to work on this audit for much longer. His messages were starting to creep over into completely rude territory. Despite her big talk to Paul on Saturday morning, Jenn still hadn't filed an official complaint against Greg. Not yet. She wanted to help Stetson save his farm or figure *something* out, and then she'd file the complaint against Greg. She didn't want to chance being pulled off the case.

An audit had never meant so much before, and yet, Jennifer had never failed so miserably.

Working Overtime started ringing out as her phone began vibrating across the scarred wooden desk. *Dammmmiiitttttt*...She did *not* want to talk to Greg right now. Or ever, for that matter, but especially not right now. Not when she didn't have much in the way of progress to report. She hesitated for a moment, trying to figure out if she could get away with not answering for once, but finally, worry won out and she snatched the phone up, hurrying to the front door as she tried to swipe to answer. The phone call went to voicemail just a split second before she could, though, and Jennifer grimaced, nibbling on her bottom lip as she looked down at the screen.

Should she call him back? Or listen to his voicemail first and then call him—

The phone started ringing again.

I don't want to work.
I want to bang on these drums all day.

Well, I guess that answers that question.

She swiped again as she stepped out onto the front porch. "This is Jennifer Kendall."

I sound more pleasant than I feel. That's a good start.

"Why didn't you answer when I called just a second ago?" Greg demanded.

"I couldn't get to the phone fast enough. It was in my bag," Jennifer lied without a twinge of guilt. She was pretty sure she should feel guilty about *not* feeling guilty, but that wasn't about to happen. Not with Greg.

"I've had just about enough of your excuses. I'm tired of reminding you that I don't want to hear them," Greg blasted her.

"It was just a reason, not an excuse," she said, keeping her voice even. She was not going to let him get under her skin. She refused to.

"I don't want to hear it. Are you done with the audit yet?" he demanded.

"I'm still working on the books. It's a complicated business, with cows and row crops and hay——"

"You've dragged your feet long enough on this one," he snapped, cutting her off. "I want an answer today, and it better be foreclosure."

"What?!" she half yelled. She knew that was what he wanted, but he rarely demanded it. "But that may not——"

"That is the answer that I want, that is the answer the board wants, and that is going to be the answer you give. You're only out there on this little vacation because the loan contract stipulates that an audit must be conducted. The contract doesn't say what the results of that audit must be. We, as the bank, get to *determine* what the result of that audit will be, and this one will be foreclosure. Do I make myself clear?"

"You know that is——"

"You don't get to tell me what to think. I am the boss, you are the employee, and therefore, I get to tell you what to think. Get me my results, and quick."

"I can't—"

"You can't what? You can't work here anymore? That is what is going to happen if you continue to be insubordinate."

"That isn't—"

"I really don't care what you think it is or isn't. Let me tell you *exactly* what it is. This is about the board backing a huge development deal to gentrify that little asshole of a town. If you haven't noticed, that farm is right at the base of the Goldfork Mountains, and with a little bit of the bank's money, it could be a very nice ski resort. If you don't want to play ball, then I don't need your services any longer. Now get me that report!"

The line went dead.

It all clicked together in that moment. His even-more-overbearing-than-usual manner. His willingness to openly demand what the results of the audit would be.

Worthwhile...

The word of the day, except this time, it was the bank that won the contest. They'd been able to figure out how to make the mountainside worthwhile, when she and Stetson hadn't.

Hold on, Stetson could sell to real estate developers instead! The bank couldn't be in possession of the only people willing and able to pay for a whole ski resort to be put in, right? They'd just have to find some backers themselves.

She groaned, burying her face in her hands. That was ridiculous, and even she knew it. These were the kinds of deals that took months or even years to put together, not a couple of days. Stetson needed cash right now, not two years from now. Plus, would he even be willing to voluntarily turn his family's farm into a ski resort?

Jennifer was pretty sure the answer to that was a resounding *hell no*, although honestly, she wasn't sure if he was going to have a choice here pretty quick.

"Is everything okay?" Carmelita asked, opening the screen door with Jennifer's favorite flowered mug in her hand. "I made you some coffee. I thought you might need it."

Jennifer took it gratefully with a wan smile. *What happens when you lose the only home you've lived in for the last 50 years? What happens when I have to tell the man I'm falling in love with that his life is about to be destroyed?*

"Yeah, I'm good," she said hoarsely. "I better get back to work, though."

She left Carmelita on the front porch, staring into the distance contemplatively as Jennifer headed back to the office.

Maybe this time, she'd have better luck. It sure as hell couldn't get any worse.

CHAPTER 42

STETSON

STETSON LOOKED UP from the puzzle they were putting together to stare at the waterfall of hair opposite him at the card table. He loved watching her think. It was like watching a whole play take place, but he was the only audience member.

Probably the only time in his life he'd be able to afford such up-close-and-personal seats to a theatre production.

"Have you seen the chimney stack yet?" Jennifer murmured, her eyes scanning the pieces on the card table between them, biting her lower lip as she searched.

Biting her lower lip…it had to be the most distracting move Jennifer could make. Every time she did it, a bolt of pure lust shot through him. He wondered if she had any idea how enticingly gorgeous she was.

Scratch that. She didn't. Not after how Paul had treated her.

Stetson figured he'd just have to be the one to show her the truth.

"You know, the puzzle pieces are on the card table," Jennifer said with a teasing lilt to her voice, even as she continued to scan the pieces in front of her. "It helps if you look down when you're trying to find the next piece to put in place."

Stetson felt his cheeks flush a bit, which he immediately decided to blame on the dark beer Carmelita had brought out for him.

He cleared his throat. "I...uhhh...haven't spotted it yet," he said truthfully, forcing himself to look down at the puzzle spread out in front of them instead of staring at Jennifer. She was way more fascinating than a generic puzzle of a farmhouse with a horse grazing in the pasture any day of the week.

He had just started to search in earnest for the missing chimney piece when Jennifer held it up triumphantly. "There you are, you little bugger," she crowed, pushing the piece into place.

"So you never told me why you thought you killed your mother," she said quietly, her eyes still trained on the puzzle as she continued to search through the pieces.

"Wha...oh. Right." He hadn't forgotten; rather, he'd hoped she'd forgotten.

He'd blurted that out in a fit of desperation, trying to distract her from being upset about Paul. He hadn't thought through the ramifications of actually telling her before it'd come spilling out.

He began pulling all of the white daisy patch pieces out of the jumble, thinking as his hands went to work. He always thought best while doing something, and he wondered for a moment if counselors had ever considered having their patients put puzzles together while talking to them, so they could think clearly enough to make progress.

"I like to think of myself as having been a pretty good kid," he said quietly, as his stack of white daisy pieces grew. "I wasn't an angel, but I wasn't intentionally destructive, either. I wasn't Declan, though. By all accounts, Declan was the easiest out of all of us. Maybe that's why he and Mom were so close." Stetson shrugged. "Or maybe Declan was just the most like my mom. Both peacemakers. Both hardworking and loyal. The way they held their heads...Declan was my mom's mini-me, while I was my dad's mini-me. Wyatt was just...Wyatt."

Jennifer looked up and watched him closely as he talked, and he shifted a bit in his seat, uncomfortable to have those brilliant green eyes focused on him. He rather wished she'd look away, but of course he'd never tell her that.

He began connecting the daisies, flipping pieces around and trying them one by one.

"I was *just* starting to hit those teenage years – you know, where hormones rule your brain – I was just twelve but there was a girl two years younger..." He let out a low whistle. "Emma Dyer was her name. She left town as soon as she graduated from high school, so you won't ever meet her, but damn. She was my first crush. You never forget your first."

He looked up to see her smiling slightly at him, listening intently as if he was telling her the most fascinating story in the world.

He plunged on.

"I wanted her to come over here so I could show off the farm – I don't know what I thought she'd want to see, since most 10-year-old girls aren't hot to trot about row cropping, but I was young and head over heels in love. It was the ponytails – just perfect for pulling." He winked at Jennifer and she laughed. "Anyway, I asked my mom if Emma could come over, and she reminded me that I hadn't done my chores yet that day. I didn't get to have fun with my friends until my chores were done.

"Well, I was pretty upset. I probably had an hour's worth of chores to do, and if I'd hurried through them, I could've had plenty of time to spend with Emma but I wasn't thinking logically, of course. I was just mad that my mom was telling me no. I told her that I hated her. Told her she was mean. I went stomping outside and promptly took about three times as long to do my chores as it should've taken, 'cause I was busy having a pity party for myself through the whole thing. When you're having a pity party, you don't exactly zip through your chores at top speed."

He felt his cheeks warm again as his eyes stung a

little. Which was ridiculous. He was a grown man. He cleared his throat, and then cleared it again.

Finally, he continued. "I never saw her again. She was on her way to Pocatello to do a surprise visit with Declan when she struck a deer just outside of Twin Falls. It took me a real long time to realize that she hadn't decided to take that trip just to get away from me and spend more time with her favorite son. I mean, who is so desperate to get away from her youngest son that she dies in the process, right?" He smiled without humor, staring at the completed daisy patch in front of him.

"Looking back on it, those two events just happened to occur on the same day. I'd been a turd, but I'd been a turd before, and I'm sure Wyatt had been an even bigger turd than that to Mom. But it…I wish I'd had a chance to tell her I was sorry. More than anything, that's what I want to tell her."

The room was quiet, the flickering candlelight on the walls adding the only life and movement to the two of them. Jennifer wasn't saying anything, and it was killing him so finally he looked up, willing to take the judgment in her eyes. He hadn't actually killed his mom, but he hadn't been nice, either, and Jennifer had every right to think badly about him because of it.

But she was staring at him, tears dripping endlessly down her face. She wasn't trying to wipe them away or hide them. They were just there. Moving ceaselessly. She gave him a tremulous smile and reached her hand out to him. "I can't imagine," she said softly. "If my mom died every time I said something to her that I didn't really mean – especially during my teenage years – I would've been charged with mass murder a long time ago. Is it mass murder if you kill the same person multiple times?"

They laughed quietly for just a moment at the macabre question.

"I'm sure your mom knew how much you loved her, even if you were your dad's mini-me. Moms love their children no matter how much we disappoint them or say awful things to them."

He nodded, swallowing hard a couple of times. She was right, of course.

"I'm just glad that Carmelita never tried to be my mom," he said softly. "She is more like my grandmother, you know? But if she'd tried to take over my mom's place, I don't know if I would've handled it well. It's kind of impressive; Carmelita has a lot of tact. She just thinks that I don't always need the watered-down version from her. She's not one to hold back."

Jennifer reached out her hand and took his in it. "Carmelita loves you very much; your parents loved you very much." She stroked her thumb over his bruised and scabbed knuckles. He'd finally been able to ditch the bandages a couple of days ago. "I'm not sure about your brothers, though."

It took him a second to realize that she was teasing him, and he jerked his head up to find her grinning at him while she wiped at her cheeks with her free hand.

"I'm not sure about my brothers either," he said with a small laugh of his own. "But I do know what I think about the rest of the people in my life." He stood up and pulled her out of her chair so he could scoop her up into his arms. He decided on the spot that all females should be made pocket-sized. It made it so much easier to get them into bed whenever he wanted them there. "I think there's a certain female with the most delicious pussy I ever did taste." He flipped off light switches with his elbow as he headed to bed, so Carmelita wouldn't be upset come morning. "In fact, I'm feeling a might bit hungry right now."

He hurried into his bedroom where he tossed her onto the bed, listening to her squeal of laughter and watching all of the right body parts bounce just like always. Now *there* was a sight he'd never get tired of seeing.

CHAPTER 43

JENNIFER

*J*ENNIFER AWOKE with a big yawn and an even bigger smile. She was damn happy that morning, although it took her a minute to remember why. Oh. Right. Stetson last night. She stretched luxuriously as she looked around the room. He must've slipped out to go check on the cows.

Well, that just meant that she could eat another one of Carmelita's amazing breakfasts and then get right to work. The clock was ticking. She'd blown past Greg's demand that her report be turned in yesterday, hoping to ride on the fact that she'd always had excellent employee evaluations, and perhaps the bank president and the board would be reluctant to let someone like her go.

But she only had hours to find a way to outsmart her boss, before the clock would run out and she would have to admit defeat. She hadn't told Stetson last night about Greg's demands on the phone yesterday, because what good would it do? It would only make him worry more, and he'd done enough worrying to last a lifetime. Now, it was all up to her.

Sleep was for wusses, *or* people who'd managed to help their boyfriend save his farm.

Boyfriend...

She paused in the middle of brushing her teeth to stare at herself in the mirror. He was her boyfriend, right? He'd never actually asked her or anything formal like that, but she was sleeping in his bed every night, and they were spending every waking moment with each other when they weren't working.

Two nights ago, he'd finally taken her over to the bustling metropolis of Franklin – she rolled her eyes to herself even as she thought the words – and as they'd wandered through downtown, checking out the adorable shops along the way, Jennifer had remembered back to when she'd first arrived in Sawyer, and how Margaret had given her lousy directions in her hunt for dinner.

That had been a lifetime ago, or at least it felt like it.

She spit out her toothpaste and rinsed her toothbrush, setting it in the holder off to the side.

It was time to do her job. It was time to help Stetson and Carmelita save their home.

Which was why, when she finally spotted the key to it all, she may or may not have thrown her hands up in the air and let out a huge whoop of delight. She threw herself out of the Fainting Goat Chair and danced around the office, happiness and relief flooding through her in equal measures. She'd done it. She'd actually damn well done it.

"What is it?" Carmelita's voice floated to her as her soft footsteps echoed through the house. She made it to the office door slightly out of breath. "Are you okay?"

"I am *great!*" she hollered, kissing Carmelita on both cheeks. "Never better! Where's Stetson?"

"Outside. He said something about counting hay bales—"

"I gotta go!" she said, too excited to let Carmelita finish. "I'll tell you all about it later!"

She dashed out of the office and down the hallway to the front door, where she slipped on her new boots from Frank's. She felt the same thrill she always felt when she pulled them on, but she pushed that down. She had to focus. She could oohh and aahh over adorable cowgirl boots later all she wanted.

Right now, she had a farm to save.

CHAPTER 44

STETSON

*H*E WAS WORKING the shovel, doing his best to dig out the curly dock while not jostling the thousands of seeds that were ready to drop at a moment's notice. The fight against curly dock was a never-ending one, but since cows getting into a patch of it could be fatal, it was a war where he was never allowed to admit defeat.

"Stetson!" He heard Jennifer's voice calling out, drifting on the wind. He looked up to see her in the distance, hurrying through the pasture as quickly as her legs would carry her, waving her arms frantically at him.

His nerves were instantly on edge. Whatever it was, it had to be important. She wouldn't be running like her ass was on fire for anything less. Good important or bad important, he'd know in a moment. He swung his shovel up over his shoulder and headed her way, his strides eating up the ground.

When she got closer, he saw she was beaming from ear to ear, and he knew instantly that it was a good important. *Thank God.* He felt his stomach muscles loosen a little. As long as no one was dead on the side of the road, he'd enjoy a break from digging up weeds any day of the week, especially if that break came in the form of a very happy Jennifer.

"Carmelita said you'd be counting hay bales," she gasped, once she got to his side.

"I was, but then——"

"Never mind!" she hollered, waving her hands around in the air. "I found it!" she said around gasps from her run across the three fields between them and the hay barn. She grinned up at him, positively radiating with joy. "I know how you can save the farm!"

Stetson stopped breathing as he stared down at her. Had she really? She'd done it? "What?!" he practically yelled. "What did you find?"

She grabbed his hands and began doing an impromptu jig with him.

"The wheat!" she hollered as she danced around him. "You can sell the 30,000 bushels of wheat!"

A ball of panic and dread bloomed instantly in Stetson's chest and he yanked his hands out of her grasp.

No, no, not the wheat!

He was already shaking his head as he began to back away from her.

CHAPTER 45

JENNIFER

*H*ER GRINNING, joyous Stetson was gone, and in its place was a stone-cold wall of...nothing. He began backing away, shaking his head as he did so.

What just happened here?

She took a few tentative steps towards him, and he held his hands up defensively. He looked...

Angry? Upset? Dead to her? She suddenly couldn't read him, and that scared her more than anything.

He dropped his hands and straightened up to his full, towering height over her. "I'm not selling the wheat," he said flatly, staring down at her.

"Wha...what?" she stuttered. Her whole world shifted to the side, cockeyed and weird and out of focus. "But...but I did the math!" she protested. "If you can find a buyer for that wheat who'll give you at least $6.25 a bushel, you can make the bank payment *and* cover the late fees. You'll be all caught up."

"I am *not* selling the wheat for less than $9 a bushel," he replied, his normally warm, brown eyes instead hard as flint. He was staring at her like...

Like she was the enemy. She'd forgotten how awful it was to have Stetson look at her like this, and honestly, when he had before, they hadn't been dating and falling in love. To see this side of him again, after everything...

She shivered despite the heat from the summer sun on her arms. How could it be so sunshine-y and bright, and yet so dark and awful at the same time? She felt like she'd been dropped down the rabbit hole. Nothing made sense. When she'd found the entry for the 30,000 bushels of wheat, but no corresponding entry for the sale of it, she was so sure she'd solved everything.

Well, he had to simply be misunderstanding her. He'd never struck her as less-than-intelligent previous to now, but she was having a hard time restraining herself from drawing pictures on the ground with the end of his shovel. Maybe a few pictographs would help things along. Hand gestures?

Something? Anything at all, really.

"Stetson," she said firmly, determined to get this conversation back on track, "if you could get the $6.25, you could get Intermountain to leave you alone."

"I saaaiiidddd," he snarled, "I am *not* selling that wheat for less than $9, and that's final! That wheat…it was the last crop my father harvested." He was walking away from her, heading for the four-wheeler parked at the edge of the field. His long legs were gobbling up the ground and she had to sprint to keep up with him. "He wanted to get at least $9 for it, and *that* is what I'm going to get!"

"So you'd rather let the grain rot in the bins and lose your father's farm," Jennifer shouted, huffing as she ran, "than sell for less than what he wanted? You…this is ridiculous!" she spat.

"It was his last wish," he snarled, chucking his shovel as hard as he could across the field before he spun on his boot heel to growl down at her, "and I'm gonna make sure it happens no matter what! You city people just don't get it. You'll *never* understand what it means to follow through on a promise." His face was as red as hers, his hands in fists at his side.

The shovel went skidding across the field before hitting a clump of grass and jamming into it. The polished wooden handle quivered a little in the summer sun.

City people…

He was hurling the worst insult he could think of at her; she knew him well enough to know that. Questioning her parentage would've been less of an insult.

What she couldn't figure out was why. Where was

this coming from? She searched his eyes, but found nothing there. Dark and oh so cold. Her Stetson was gone and she had *no* idea how to get him back.

Her mind spun in circles. How could she reach him? She *had* to get through to him.

"If...if you don't sell the wheat," she warned him, stabbing him in the chest with her forefinger, "I'm gonna have to recommend that the bank foreclose on the farm."

He said nothing.

"Stetson, you're forcing me into a corner!" she cried. How could he do this? What the hell was going on in that head of his?

"Fine, take it!" he erupted. "It's what you wanted all along. All this bullshit about helping people was just an act!"

"*What?!* Is that what you really think?" Jennifer tried to hold back the tears, but they were just as angry as the rest of her. They leaked out of her eyes and scorched streaks down her face. She hated that she cried when she was angry. She wasn't sad right now; she was pissed. So why did her eyes insist on crying?

Some days, she damn well hated being a girl.

"*I* think," he hollered, jabbing himself in the chest with his thumb, "that everyone wants me to leave this farm, so why shouldn't I? My brothers wanted me to leave, Michelle wanted me to leave, and now the bank wants me to leave. So just take the damn thing!"

His long legs covered the last few feet to the four-wheeler and then tires were spraying dirt and grass clumps as he tore off, leaving his shovel behind. She watched him go, the endless tears trailing down her face.

CHAPTER 46

JENNIFER

S HE PACED the front porch of the farmhouse as she tried to reason through her choices, wiping angrily at her eyes with every pass. Honestly, though, what choice did she have left?

Not a one. Not with Stetson the Stubborn pulling stupid stunts like this.

Hmmm…maybe she would change that to Stetson the Stubborn Shithead. It had a nice alliteration to it, even if it wasn't a nickname she could use around Carmelita.

Finally, her shoulders drooped in defeat. What she'd told him was true – he really was backing her into a corner. She couldn't sell his wheat for him; she couldn't find a group of real estate investors in the next thirty minutes who were willing to back a ski resort; and she sure as hell wasn't going to be able to dig up a wheelbarrow full of semi-precious stones from the Goldfork Mountains and find buyers willing to pay cash for them.

This was it. This was his only *worthwhile* choice, and he was throwing it all away.

She was hurt and bewildered and angry and pissed as hell.

She was damn glad Carmelita couldn't read thoughts, because if she saw the swear words that Jennifer was using right now in her mind...well, she'd probably change her mind about wanting to see the two of them together. Not that it mattered, of course. Men didn't tend to date women who were busy recommending that their farm be taken away from them, and women didn't tend to date men who were dumber than a fencepost.

So yeah, it was fair to call their relationship toast. Finished. Kaput.

Stupid Stetson the Stubborn Shithead.

Heh. Even better.

Jennifer was relieved to find that Mike the Mechanic answered the phone on the second ring, *and* that her car was finished. She hadn't worried about what was going on with it before, because honestly, where had she needed to go? Anywhere she had wanted to go, she had wanted to go there with Stetson.

But now...well, she needed to go far, far away, and she sure as hell wasn't taking Stetson along for the ride. Jennifer had never met Mike, but his warm gravelly voice was the one steady rock in her world right now, and she clung to it for all that she was worth.

Mike told her that Stetson had left his credit card on file to pay for the damage, and in the mood she was in, all she could think was that he'd better sell some of that damned wheat so he'd have enough money to pay off the credit card bill when it showed up. He wasn't willing to sell it to save the family farm, but maybe he'd be willing to sell it to pay a piddling credit card bill.

Well, not her problem anymore, right?

Mike assured her that he was happy to deliver the Honda out to the farm and thought he could have it to her in about an hour.

Thanking the man, she ended the call before heading upstairs to pack her things. She threw everything into her suitcase, a jumble of clothes and makeup and toiletries, but for once, she didn't care. Usually a fastidious packer, the tears streaming unchecked down her cheeks made it hard to see and even harder to give a damn.

When the body shop man showed up at the farm with her car, she signed the paperwork by Braille. She never looked the man in the eye, letting her hair cover her face, afraid he'd see the trail of tears cascading endlessly down – a personal version of the Niagara Falls. She tried not to snuffle too much, but she wasn't sure she was fooling anyone.

Carmelita didn't seem to be in the house, and for that, Jennifer was eternally grateful. She didn't know how to explain what had happened to the housekeeper, mostly because she didn't know herself. She kept blinking and looking around, fully expecting to wake up from this nightmare. It *was* just a nightmare, right?

But she wasn't waking up and she didn't know how to function in this new world, this new reality she found herself in.

Even as her mind was following the same loop that went nowhere, frantically running in place and gaining nothing, she couldn't help scolding herself for her hero complex she'd somehow taken on. She thought she could solve a problem that no one else could. She thought she'd found something that Stetson had somehow overlooked.

A silo full of threshed and cleaned wheat? Had she really been so naïve and eager for a happy ending that she'd assume that he would completely forget about 30,000 bushels of wheat? He was a stubborn asshole, not an amnesiatic asshole, for hell's sakes.

She thought back through their tour of the farm. He'd never mentioned the silos, although it was hard to miss them, considering how gigantic they were. She'd been the one to bring them up, asking him what was stored in them. He'd said wheat, after it was harvested, and then...they were talking about something else. Smooth as butter. Never missed a beat.

He'd absolutely known about the wheat, had been reminded about the wheat in case he'd somehow forgotten, and still chose to keep it to himself. The one thing that would save five generations of Miller's work and sweat and tears from the grasp of a bank wanting to develop a high-end ski resort.

How? Just...how? That was what kept tripping her up. She hated things that didn't make sense, that didn't fit into her neat columns and rows in an Excel sheet.

She found that she kept bouncing between mad as a wet cat, and heartbroken that she was leaving Stetson behind. Or, more accurately, she was heartbroken to leave what she thought they had behind.

His eyes, brown and warm and caring, telling her how beautiful she was to him. His eyes, brown and vulnerable and hurting, telling her how he wished he could just tell his mother he was sorry.

Sorry...

Never once, through everything that had happened between them, had he ever actually said the words, "I'm sorry" to her. He'd gotten close, but to Jennifer's new way of thinking, close only counted with hand grenades and horseshoes. From here forward, she wasn't going to put up with a man who refused to admit when he was wrong.

In fact, Stupid Stetson the Stubborn Shithead better be ready to downright *grovel* if he ever wanted to speak to her again. She'd accept nothing less. She deserved nothing less.

That was, if he ever did want to speak to her again.

The tears ran faster down her face.

She could only be grateful that traffic was light, because she honestly couldn't remember much about the actual drive back to Boise. Pine trees and rocky hillsides and a deep ravine with a rushing river cascading through it ran alongside the road, but it was just there. Picturesque scenery flying by that she'd normally be oohing and aahing over, but now...

She just couldn't care.

By the time she reached the outskirts of Boise, she was completely numb, a state of being she was happy to embrace. She didn't want to feel or worry or think.

A part of her – a tiny part of her that she just couldn't bring herself to listen to – was trying to warn her that she needed to go into work. Greg was probably frantic by this point. She had no doubt that he'd called her a half dozen times just that morning, but she'd turned her phone off hours ago.

If he wanted to talk to her, he could listen to her happy, professional, upbeat voicemail message and have a discussion with her there. She could give him nothing more than that; she had nothing else to give.

She crawled into bed, pulled the covers up over her head, and embraced the darkness. Here, nothing could hurt her.

Sometime later – hours, weeks, months, she couldn't tell – she rolled over and pulled her phone out of her laptop bag, where she'd thrown it on the floor when she'd come home. She turned it on, waiting for the Apple logo to disappear and the phone to come to life. The clock on her nightstand said 6:32, but she didn't know if it was 6:32 at night, or 6:32 in the morning.

Finally, her phone was alive. It was 6:32 in the morning, and it was Friday. That meant...she forced her brain to work, scrambling to put times together... she'd been hiding in bed for a little over twelve hours.

No wonder her bladder hurt so much.

She forced herself to make a trip to the bathroom, and then she snuggled back down in the bed. It was safe here. No one could touch her.

The part of her brain that was yelling at her to deal with the shitty situation she'd found herself in was yelling louder, though. It was right – she did need to do something.

So she did.

Ignoring the eleven voicemails from her boss, she called into the HR department for the bank and left a voicemail, stating that she'd caught a cold and didn't want to pass it along to others. She'd be back to work on Monday. Considering how obnoxiously awful she sounded in that moment, her throat raw from crying and cursing Stetson's stupidity, she was pretty sure they would believe her.

If only it was true. She would have much rather had a cold than a broken heart. A cold would go away. This...never would.

She laid there and thought about calling Bonnie

to whine and cry her heart out, but the idea of having to explain it all to someone else…she was too tired. She would explain it later. When she could move and think and breathe again without pain.

Plus, Bonnie had to go to work. She couldn't just sit around and act like a human Kleenex, soaking up all of the pain inside of Jennifer.

No, it was better to just keep this to herself. She'd already forced Bonnie to live through the tail-end of one break-up with a boyfriend. She wouldn't force her to live through two.

CHAPTER 47

JENNIFER

By lunchtime on Monday, her finger hung over the keyboard like the blade of a guillotine. Her hand slowly lowered and her eyes closed on their own. She felt her finger make contact.

Well, I guess that's it.

She'd done it. She'd filed the damn report that would take the farm away from Stetson the Shithead and Carmelita the Cind. Karmelita the Kind?

Hmmmm…that alliteration wasn't exactly working out the way she'd wanted it to.

She waved the hazy thoughts away. Everything was in a haze, really. She tried to care about the world around her, but it was like peering through cloudy glass, covered in hard water deposits. It was there, but not.

Greg had been buzzing her office every 30 minutes since she'd shuffled through the front door that morning. He was, of course, threatening that if she didn't send him that report right away, he'd fire her on the spot, which had the unexpected result of making her laugh out loud. He was making the fatal assumption that she gave a damn.

She didn't.

She'd hung up, listening to his tinny voice let out a blistering tirade all the way down into the phone cradle, and then his voice was gone.

She wished it was that easy to get rid of him in real life.

But, she'd finally done what he was demanding – the only thing she could do under the circumstances. For once, this wasn't Greg's fault. She couldn't point her finger at him and ask him how dare he do what he was doing. No, the only report she could give to the bank just happened to also be the report that would make Greg happy.

Some days, life sucked.

Pressing the intercom button, Jennifer buzzed the receptionist.

"Susan, Greg is going to buzz my line – again – in a few minutes. Will you be kind enough to tell him that the report is in his inbox and that I have gone home sick?"

Back to my bed, to darkness, to where nothing can hurt me. After having spent three days hiding in bed, she was finding that she didn't like the outside world all that much. She wanted her cocoon back.

"Actually, you can't leave just yet. You have an appointment. A client called this morning and asked to meet with you today; he said it was urgent. He's here now. Should I send him back?"

I swear to God, if Paul walks through that door, there is no way I am not going to jail today.

"Yeah, send him back," she said heavily, before taking a deep breath and putting on her happy customer service face.

A man stopped just inside her office door, a bouquet of flowers covering his face.

Jennifer froze, and for the second time that week, her whole world shifted to the side, cockeyed and weird and out of focus. This couldn't be…it wasn't…

But even with the flowers covering his face, Jennifer absolutely knew who it was.

But I just sent that report! Oh Stetson, you're too late! Too late by only minutes, but no, that wasn't true because even if he was bringing her flowers, that didn't mean he was also coming to pay off the farm, so actually, minutes, hours, days, it didn't matter when he came with flowers.

He'd forced her to ruin his life, and she wasn't sure who would hate who more once that came out – if she'd hate him more for making her do it, or if he'd hate her more for actually doing it.

"What…" Her voice cracked and she cleared her throat to try again. *Do not cry!* "What are you doing here?"

He slowly lowered the flowers until she could see his dark brown eyes, warm and haunted and worried, but she could read him again. He wasn't looking at her like she was the enemy.

Not yet.

"I came to tell you…" He paused, swallowing hard, shifting from foot to foot as he stared at her. "I came to say that I am sorry."

He said it. She couldn't believe he'd actually said it.

She blinked. The swirl of emotions inside of her was overwhelming everything and she just froze in place.

"Have you ever watched the movie *Love Story*?" Stetson asked, apropos of absolutely nothing whatsoever.

She blinked.

"Made in the 1970s; an adaptation from a book?" he prodded her.

She finally shook her head. She felt slightly ill. Was this a hallucination? She felt like she might be hallucinating. It was the weirdest hallucination ever, but then again, wasn't that kinda the definition of a hallucination?

"My dad loved that movie," Stetson said, not moving a muscle, holding the flowers, just standing there as he talked. "Rough 'n tumble farmer, but he thought *Love Story* was the best thing since sliced bread."

She blinked.

"There's a line at the end of it. The guy tells his dad, 'Love means never having to say you're sorry.'

That's how I was raised. My dad took pride in never telling us kids that he was wrong, or sorry, or that he'd screwed something up. You know how I told you that my dad said that I was his do-over, his chance to do things better than he had with Declan and Wyatt?"

She nodded numbly.

"He never told them that. He only told me. If he'd told them that, then he would've had to admit to their faces that he'd made a mistake in his life. My parents were married for 22 years. My dad never once told my mom he was sorry, because he'd never been wrong, you see." He gave a sarcastic twist of the lips to that idea.

"I might just have more pride than my dad, and I promise you, that's saying somethin'. I've only ever said I was sorry to my brothers, and it was only after I was beaten with a belt into doing it.

"But Jennifer…I'm sorry. More sorry than I have the words for." His cheeks flushed red, and his eyes seemed to take on a suspicious sparkle, as if they were filling with tears.

Jennifer was willing to bet her right arm that he cried even less often than he said he was sorry.

Suddenly, her gaze jerked to her office door, where people were walking past, discussing interest rates and what the bond market was going to do…He moved out of the way as she hurried to the door and shut it, leaning against it for support as she stared up at Stetson. She didn't exactly want the entire office to hear this discussion.

And then, she waited for him to go on.

She'd told herself that he'd have to grovel before she took him back, and she'd meant it. Although finally telling her he was sorry was a real nice place to start, it didn't excuse everything else away.

It didn't make everything better.

"I miss my dad more every day," he whispered, a trickle of moisture spilling out of his left eye, the light green bruises the only remnant of the fight he'd had with Wyatt. "I thought it was hard when he passed, but sometimes, ignorance is bliss. I didn't know what I didn't know, until he was gone. He'd tried one time to talk to me about bills and taxes and insurance, and I'd told him not to worry about it, because he wasn't going anywhere. I wouldn't listen to him. I don't know if I was more terrified by him dying, or me actually being left in charge of all of that. Unfortunately, they went hand-in-hand."

He laid the bouquet down on the guest chair opposite her desk, and used his freed hands to dash the tears away that were running down his cheeks. He stared at the door over her shoulder as he continued quietly, "It's stupid to have put so much emotion into a damn crop. Somehow, in my mind, it became so much more than just a pile of wheat. It was actually the last of my dad, and it meant letting him go. Once it was sold, I'd have nothing left to hold onto.

"You know, other than the recliner in the family room, the Fainting Goat Chair in his office, and pretty much every tool and piece of equipment on the farm." He rolled his eyes at himself. "Wanna know why I didn't get a new office chair, even though that one has fallen over on me a couple of times? Because my dad used that one. Wanna know why I didn't switch to a closer bank than Intermountain? Because Intermountain was where my dad banked. For the past year, I've been clinging to everything I could, not wanting to let go or admit that he was truly gone.

"Luke called me an idiot, by the way." She jerked her head, startled by the comment. Stetson gave her a wry smile before going back to staring at the door. "He's my best friend. We joke that we've been friends since we were in the womb. His mom and my mom were pregnant at the same time. Anyway," he waved his hand, brushing that aside to the side, "Luke doesn't pull punches. If he thinks you're being an idiot, he'll tell you that you're being an idiot. It's one of the many reasons that we're best friends. He's my kind of blunt.

"But he told me that I needed to pull my head out of my ass, because if my dad were here, he'd be telling me the same thing. My dad didn't beat me with a belt after I got taller than him, but Luke said that for this, he probably would've at least given it his best shot. Luke is right, of course. My dad would never want me to give up the Miller Family Farm because of some sentimental attachment to *wheat*, for God's sake."

His eyes, red and swollen, dropped from the door to hers. "So, I'm here. I want you to know that I know that I screwed up. I am openly and plainly admitting that I was wrong, and I am genuinely sorry for reacting the way I did. You were just trying to help, and I treated you like shit. I don't deserve your forgiveness, but someday, I hope you'll see your way to giving it to me."

"Oh Stettttsssoonnnn…" she cried, and her heart, already stomped and broken up into a million little pieces, broke completely apart. Her legs gave way and she slid down the door, collapsing into a pile on the floor where the tears just poured out of her.

How she could still be crying was beyond her. She'd never cried so much in all her life as she had in the last four days. And yet, somehow, they still came.

His arms wrapped around her and he rocked her, back and forth. "I'm sorry, I'm sorry, I didn't mean to make you cry," he whispered into her hair. "Please don't cry. I'm sorry."

"*I'm* sorry," she hiccuped. He was never going to forgive her. *Never.* "I sent the report recommending foreclosure right before you showed up. Stetson, they're taking your farm away." She dissolved into a puddle of tears.

"Well, that explains that," he said, a bit of an ironic lilt to his voice.

She pulled away from his soaked chambray shirt to stare up at him. He'd lost his ever-lovin' mind. The stress of it all broke him.

He looked down at her with a small, self-satisfied grin. "When I handed the check over to cover my delinquent payment in full, plus fees, your boss looked like he was about to have an epileptic seizure."

"You…hold on, *what?!*" she burst out. Now she was the one losing her mind, and hearing things. Things that he couldn't possibly be saying.

"Well, after Luke gave me the kick in the ass that I needed, I didn't just sit around all weekend, trying to find the guts to tell you I'm sorry, although I will admit that I did have to really work myself up to that. No, I also called a grain buyer buddy of mine and explained the situation. He gave me $6.45 a bushel. He said the extra twenty cents was a bonus for all of the years my father was a loyal customer. Anyway, that gave me enough to come current on the loan, with just enough leftover for the flowers."

I am so in love with this man.

She launched herself at him, showering him with kisses and running her fingers through his hair, wanting to make sure it was real. He was real. It was all real.

"Greg kept ranting about some damn ski resort when I handed him the check," Stetson said between kisses. "Do you know what he was talking about? I'm wondering if he's a little screwy upstairs. I own a cattle ranch and row cropping farm. There is no ski resort on my place, or Sawyer at all. That tourist shit can't be found until you get past Franklin, thank God. Do you think he's lost his mind?"

"I'll tell you all about it later, I promise," Jennifer said, a bubble of happiness welling up inside of her, spilling out into giddy laughter. "I can't believe you did this. Oh *Stetson…*"

Which was when their kissing finally became serious for the first time. She flung herself at him, wrapping her arms around him and kissing him so deeply, the world disappeared. When they finally pulled apart, she was breathless.

"What do you think of the flowers?" Stetson asked, tilting his head toward the chair. *Oh. Right!* Somehow, among everything else, she'd forgotten about them. Getting up off the floor, she saw Stetson following her lead as she picked up the bouquet to bury her face into the bundle of red roses offset by white Calla lilies. The scent of roses filled her nose and made her head spin.

"I even wrote the card myself," he said proudly. She found the card, stamped with a logo from some place called Happy Petals, and read the words to herself. There were only two words on the card, but still, she didn't understand them.

"Will you…?" was all that was written.

Will she *what?* Her mind stumbled over a million possible answers in about a half a second.

Suddenly, she realized the card was tied to the flowers by a brown, loosely twisted string, and something was weighing the string down. She pulled the card to the side and saw, dangling from the string, a gold ring with a lovely, if small, diamond, sliding slowly along toward the stems of the flowers.

"Turns out, I had enough to bring my loan

current, buy flowers, *and* buy a ring," he said, trying to smile confidently, but she could tell his nerves were drawn taut.

Her eyes dropped back down to the ring, sliding on the string. It unleashed a cascade of conflicting thoughts that rushed through her brain so quickly, she felt dizzy.

Could I? Should I? What would I lose? What would I gain? Is he really the one?

She felt like the words were blazing on a movie screen above her head. Each question was flashing on the screen and then another piled on top, the words laying on top of each other, hard to read, hard to know what to do, and then suddenly, like a wrecking ball crashing through the side of a building, came a bold *YES!*, scattering the other words in its wake.

"I guessed at the size," Stetson said, filling the silence that must've been killing him. She slapped him on the chest playfully.

"There for a moment, you were all romantic and stuff. Don't you dare ruin this for me, Stetson Byron Miller," she said, before draping her arms around his neck. The flowers knocked his cowboy hat to one side. Laughing together, their lips met.

Finally, pulling away from his lips, she tightened her arms around his neck and with her mouth close to his ear, she whispered her answer.

"Yes. But," she pulled away, putting a finger to his lips to stop whatever he was about to say, "darlin', you need to know – love means that you *do* say you're sorry. In fact, bending and growing together, admitting faults, working to always improve…that's love to me. If that's not love to you, then this won't work. I don't need you to grovel every time you let out a fart," he laughed uproariously at that, "but I'm not gonna put up with this half-ass shit. You did it a couple of times while I was there on the farm – came right up on the words 'I'm sorry' but refused to actually say them. I won't marry someone who is gonna spend the rest of our lives trying to pretend that he's done nothing wrong."

He looped his hands around her lower back, snuggling her up against the juncture of his thighs, as he looked down at her with a quiet pride. "I bet Old Jennifer never would've dared to give Paul that lecture," he said with a grin. "Damn, I'm proud of you, and I agree with you a hundred percent. I won't say that I'm perfect, but…well, I should probably tell you now that Carmelita is on a warpath. She's called me some Spanish swear words that I didn't even know she knew. If I don't bring you back home with me, she may not let me in the house."

Jennifer let out a half-hysterical laugh, the kind of laugh that only happens after a period of stupidly high stress. "Are you trying to say that you only want me to marry you 'cause otherwise, your housekeeper won't let you back inside your own house?"

"I figure there's other side benefits too," he said, snuggling her tighter up against him. She felt him harden against her belly and when her eyes snapped up to his, he grinned down at her lasciviously. She shook her head in mock disapproval and he just laughed.

And then he grew serious.

"Jenn, I love you more than anything in the world. I love you more than my truck, my housekeeper, my family farm, even my pride. The only thing that's kept me going these last few days has been knowing that if I pulled my head out of my ass and worked hard, I just *might* have a chance at winning you back. I've done a lot of really stupid things in my life, but this has taken the cake. If you'll have me, warts and all, I promise to do all that I can to make you happy. And I promise to apologize when I'm wrong. No matter how much it sucks, it's much worse to lose you."

Jennifer savored another long look at this strong, warm-hearted, and loving man before turning to her desk and pressing a button.

"Susan, when Greg calls again, will you tell him I quit?"

EPILOGUE

JENNIFER

September, 2016

SIGHING, she sat back down at the worn kitchen table that was covered with magazines, fabric swatches, brochures, and pictures. An only child, Jennifer's mother seemed to have taken an almost unholy interest in the wedding plans and was driving down every weekend from Boise to "help" with the process. Six weeks into it, and Jennifer was already starting to go a little crazy.

The really good news was, Carmelita didn't seem to mind the mess considering the reason for it. The bad news was, Stetson had become accustomed to Carmelita's "normal" level of perfected cleanliness and the disarray had started to get to him. His barn could be a mess all day long, but the house was a whole different matter.

Truth was, this was really out-of-hand even by

Jennifer's estimation. She needed to rein in some of the chaos, but she couldn't seem to make a decision on anything, much to her mother's chagrin. She needed to talk to Stetson.

She braced her elbows on the table, crinkling some of the cake decorator brochures she'd picked up at the bridal show in Boise two weeks ago. She'd started off wanting to keep every scrap of paper that was ever considered, but now, she just didn't care.

"We could catch a flight to Vegas," Stetson said.

Jennifer flew out of her seat in surprise. She was so absorbed in all of this stuff, she hadn't heard the back door open or close. She hadn't heard his boots clicking against the tile, or the fridge door open and close, as was evidenced by the beer he was holding.

"Holy…" she panted. "Stetson, honey, don't ever sneak up on me like that again. You have to actually get married before you can kill me off with a heart attack and get the insurance."

He smiled. She loved that smile, the twinkle in his eye, and the way the left side of his mouth lifted just a little bit higher than the right. All of this magically made some of her stress disappear. She grinned up at him.

"To be fair, I, in no way, tried to sneak. I even let the screen door close on its own behind me," he said, and cracked open the beer. "Want one? I could pour you some wine."

"No, but thank you," she said and pressed on. "I really need to talk to you about the wedding."

"Babe, I already told you – it's fall," Stetson said, his smile wilting a bit. "That means harvest time. I know it's hard for you to not have me involved, but when I only get one or two paychecks a year, this is do-or-die for me. I'll help you more after I'm done and have more free time, promise."

She just stared up at him. Logically, she knew this was his busy time and that was part of what she'd signed up for when she agreed to be the wife of a farmer. Emotionally though, she needed to be the center of his attention. Just for a few moments.

Stetson looked at her and seemed to sense her conflict. For having been raised around a bunch of men with only Carmelita as a feminine example, Stetson was amazingly considerate.

"I'm here now. Maybe we could decide on one thing together before I head for a shower and then bed? What do you think we should decide on – cake? Centerpieces?"

"The date," she said, taking her opportunity by the horns. "I think we should move the date up. I think we should move it to October 2nd."

"Honey," Stetson said, sitting in the chair next to her. "I'm too busy to get married in December – what makes you think I have enough time to get married at the beginning of October? That is smack-dab in the middle of harvest. We can *maybe* move it to the weekend before Thanksgiving if you want it sooner, but even that's a real stretch for me. I know you haven't lived through a harvest before, but my days only get longer before they get shorter. You think I'm gone a lot right now – just wait until October hits. Some nights, it's just easier to sleep in the tractor than it is to come home."

"I just think the sooner the better," she said, willing herself not to cry. "I think the beginning of October is the longest we should wait."

"That just isn't possible, Jenn. We haven't even started harvest over at Declan's place because he's helping Wyatt, and Declan's place is *huge*. Plus, I want him to be there for my wedding – he's my best man, after all. I know it's tough, but that date would shut down two farms."

She couldn't hold it in any longer. At first, it was just a tear on her cheek but before she could even try to get a handle on her emotions, she was blubbering and sobbing. Stetson pulled her to him and stroked her hair.

He waited until she'd gotten most of the lip-sucking under control before asking, "Why is this so important?"

"The…the…the drahhh…the dress," she finally blurted out before the sobbing took over again.

Stetson held her again until she got a better grip on her waterworks.

"The dress? I thought that was the one thing that was decided."

She wiped the tears away with the back of her sleeve.

"It is. It's here already."

"So what's the problem?"

"It won't fit," she said, and then stopped. She wasn't really sure what to say.

"Ah, damn," Stetson said, the relief at finding a simple solution registering on his face and in his voice. "Can you send it back? Or hell, just buy a new one."

"I don't know what size I'll be by then," she said miserably. She had no idea how blunt she was going to have to be, and even more worrisome, she had *no* idea what his reaction was going to be.

"Why not?" he asked. He obviously hadn't connected the dots.

She couldn't find the right way to say it. She was pretty sure he would be happy, but there was a real chance that all of this was happening way too fast for him, *and* was happening at the time of year where all he did was concentrate on bringing the harvest in.

She knew that was part of the problem, too. If she had to say it outright, she wanted the announcement to be perfect. She wanted this to be one of those moments that was just right. She just couldn't find that perfect phrasing in her head.

Stetson's mind made the connection before she found those perfect words.

"You're not...?" he said, his eyes widening. "Are you really? Are we going to have a..."

She nodded her head.

"Yeeehaaaaa!" Stetson yelled.

Vaulting out of his chair, he began to dance with joy around the kitchen. She couldn't help giggling as she watched him skip and twirl around the cooking island. He was laughing so hard, tears were running down his cheeks.

Carmelita rushed into the room, fear written across her face, fear that quickly changed to an all-consuming confusion. Stetson pranced and skipped over to the short woman. He surprised her even more by picking her up by the waist and spinning her around.

Stetson set Carmelita back on her feet after a couple of turns, her face still a frozen mask of shock.

Jennifer watched in surprise as he grabbed Carmelita's cheeks and squeezed.

"We're having a father! I'm going to be a baby," he yelled, whooping happily before planting a big kiss on her forehead as Jennifer doubled over with laughter. "You're going to be a grandma!"

Well, I guess he got the gist of it.

∾

Quick Author's Note

FOR SOME OF you who weren't around when I was originally struggling to make it as a western romance author, you might not know that the original version of *Accounting for Love* was actually written by my husband.

No, seriously. **My husband wrote a romance**

novel. How many husbands do you know who would write a *romance* novel?!

Granted, it was filled to the brim with detailed crop rotation information and how you can't follow a "needy crop" like corn with another "needy crop" like…

.

.

Sorry, what? I was zoning out and didn't hear what you were blathering on about.

Okay, so the truth is, I've lived in Idaho much of my life and even *I* know virtually nothing about crop rotation, and I fully plan on keeping it that way, thankyouverymuch.

So of course, I told him he had to lose all of that, and of course, he told me that I was dead wrong.

(Don't tell me you didn't see that one coming!)

Considering he'd read like two romance novels *ever*, and I'd spent, oh I don't know, *my entire life* since about the age of 12 devouring them one right after another, you can imagine how well this certitude on my husband's behalf went over. 😉

After *ahem* a *spirited* discussion (or seven) I finally convinced him to drop all of the farming deets (or at least most of them) and I also worked hard on cleaning up the writing, and I changed this and added that and edited this and…

I eventually published *Accounting for Love* in the fall of 2016 and although I liked it, it was this weird blend of Me + Husband, rather than just Me.

In other words, I didn't *love* it.

I wrote more books and the world of Long Valley grew, and as my writing talents got stronger, my worry about *Accounting for Love* got stronger too. The better I got, the worse this book was looking in the rearview mirror, and considering that this was the very first book in a world that I planned on writing in for years to come, it only made sense for me to rewrite it.

So after months of dithering about Should I / Shouldn't I, I finally sat down in the early months of 2018 and got to work.

The book you finished today is the rewritten version. It's about 50% longer than the original version, and about 75% of it is brand new; 25% of it is recycled. Although I'm not going to say that it's a perfect book (seriously, what book is??), I will say that I like it a hell of lot more than I did before, and that I'm glad I made the decision that I did. I obviously can't keep going back and rewriting all of my books as the whim strikes, but this one really was a Must Do.

Honestly, in the end, it was a decision that was pretty much made *for* me, and I can finally say that I'm **proud** of Stetson and Jennifer's story (and Carmelita – you can't forget her!)

As I alluded to above, Long Valley is a world I plan on writing in for years to come. This is one of the best parts about writing romance novels for me – I never have to say goodbye to anyone! All of the people you just met show up in future novels – Jennifer and Stetson have a baby shower where

Stetson finally finds out if they're having a girl or a boy. Wyatt finally meets his match and learns how not to be a dickhead. Carmelita makes amazing food and lectures Stetson for swearing.

Basically, nothing ever changes, and it's really fun because although you're meeting new people and new couples are falling in love in every book, you're also meeting up with old friends too, and so it's like a high school class reunion in every book.

Well, if high school class reunions were actually fun, that is, instead of anxiety-inducing horrid get-togethers where you ask yourself what on earth made you say yes to attending it.

Or maybe it's just my class reunions that are really, really awful.

ahem

Moving right along…

I know y'all haven't had enough of Jennifer and Stetson yet, so I'm gonna treat you to a sneak peek of Book 2 in my Long Valley series, *Blizzard of Love*. It's their first Christmas together, and a blizzard shows up and best friends show up and electricity shuts off and there's a pair of red lacy panties involved…

You'll just have to keep reading to see what I'm blathering on about! 😊

Here's to many more years of loving Long Valley together,

Erin Wright

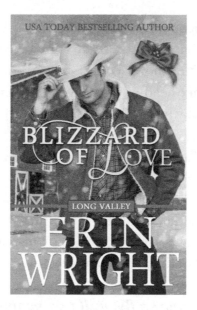

BLIZZARD OF LOVE

LONG VALLEY

ERIN WRIGHT

BLIZZARD OF LOVE

A country boy who hates Christmas for a reason, dammit...

When Luke Nash runs into Stetson Miller down at the feed store, he never expects his best friend to strong-arm him into spending Christmas at the Miller farm. Luke has no patience for Christmas cheer or Yuletide song. And the rugged cowboy *definitely* has no desire to kiss a girl under the mistletoe. No matter how infuriatingly pretty she might be.

A city girl who loves Christmas...

Bonnie Patterson adores Christmas, so when her

best friend Jennifer invites her to spend Christmas at the Miller farm, she jumps at the chance. When she sets out for the snowy country town, she has visions dancing in her head of cozy nights by a crackling fire, *not* of a hot cowboy with an ice-cold heart.

The Storm of the Century...

Instead of a peaceful holiday in the country, Bonnie gets stranded at the Miller farm by a blizzard. Even worse, she's snowed-in with Luke, an arrogant, impossible, but damn sexy cowboy.

When the sparks fly, will two people who are oh-so-different find their own Christmas miracle?

∾

Read on for a taste of *Blizzard*...

BLIZZARD OF LOVE PREVIEW

LUKE

LUKE PULLED UP in front of the old Miller farmhouse, the Christmas lights that were lining the roofline sparkling in the snow covering the landscape. It looked so festive, so Christmassy and shit.

So unlike his own house.

Sticks jumped down from the bed of the truck, his stocky Labrador body navigating the snowdrifts with ease. Luke and Stick's noses wiggled in the crisp night air, breathing in the smell of...was that pot roast?

God, it's gonna be nice to eat Carmelita's cooking this weekend. I might end up as fat as Stetson when she's done with me! Oh, but it'll be worth it.

He knocked once and then, brushing his feet on the welcome mat, pushed open the front door. "I'm here," he called out. Sticks shook the snow off his fur and then trotted in behind him.

"Hello!" Carmelita came bustling into the entryway, the delicious pot roast and...something else trailing in behind her, like the world's best smelling perfume. *Is that cinnamon rolls? I'm pretty sure it's cinnamon rolls.*

His stomach rumbled its agreement.

"Oh, you poor thing," Carmelita said in her heavily accented English, taking his jacket and hanging it up in the hall closet. "Dinner will be done soon. You go upstairs and I will tell Stetson and Jennifer you are here."

She bustled off before he could answer, and so he headed up the stairs and down to the far guest bedroom. It was a little less…girly and shit than the other one, so it was the one he usually chose when he spent the night at the Miller's house.

He lay down on the bed for a few minutes, closing his eyes and turning the idea of doing absolutely nothing for an entire weekend over and over again in his mind. This was something he hadn't done in years. Was he even capable of doing nothing for an entire weekend? He didn't know.

Dammit, am I really only 26 years old? I sound like an old man. Time to stop wallowing in my geriatric ways and get moving.

He decided to take a quick detour to the bathroom before heading downstairs, but when he slid the pocket door open, he saw something that he was pretty sure he'd never, *ever* forget: A half-naked woman, jeans down around her knees, and the most sexy pair of red lace underwear on that he'd ever seen.

It was only then that he registered a screaming noise, and realized it was because of him. She was screaming at *him*.

A whole lot of not-very-nice words.

Available at your favorite retailer or library – pick your copy up today!

ALSO BY ERIN WRIGHT

~ LONG VALLEY ~

Accounting for Love

Blizzard of Love

Arrested by Love

Returning for Love

Christmas of Love

Overdue for Love

Bundle of Love

Lessons in Love

Baked with Love

Bloom of Love (2021)

Holly and Love (TBA)

Banking on Love (TBA)

Sheltered by Love (TBA)

Conflicted by Love (TBA)

~ FIREFIGHTERS OF LONG VALLEY ~

Flames of Love

Inferno of Love

Fire and Love

Burned by Love

ABOUT ERIN WRIGHT

USA Today Bestselling author Erin Wright has worked every job under the sun, including library director, barista, teacher, website designer, and ranch hand helping brand cattle, before settling into the career she's always dreamed about: Author.

She still loves coffee, doesn't love the smell of cow flesh burning, and has embarked on the adventure of a lifetime, traveling the country full-time in an RV. (No one has died yet in the confined 250-square-foot space – which she considers a real win – but let's be real, next week isn't looking so good...)

Find her updates on ErinWright.net, where you can sign up for her newsletter along with the requisite pictures of Jasmine the Writing Cat, her kitty cat muse and snuggle buddy extraordinaire.

Wanna get in touch?
www.erinwright.net
erin@erinwright.net

Or reach out to Erin on your favorite social media platform:

facebook.com/AuthorErinWright

twitter.com/erinwrightlv

pinterest.com/erinwrightbooks

goodreads.com/erinwright

bookbub.com/profile/erin-wright

instagram.com/authorerinwright